THE HAUNTED SUITCASE AND OTHER STORIES

Colin Thompson was born in London and lived there for twenty-five years before moving to Spain, and then to a tiny island in the Outer Hebrides where he started a pottery and two of his three daughters were born.

He spent twenty years living in a remote farm-house near Hadrian's Wall before moving to Sydney, Australia in 1995. He has worked in the theatre and as a television and film director, been a weaver, a printer and a graphic artist. Since 1991 he has worked full time as an author and illustrator.

Also by the same author:

Sid the Mosquito
Attila the Bluebottle
Venus the Caterpillar
A Giant Called Norman Mary
The Paperbag Prince
Pictures of Home
Looking for Atlantis
Ruby
How to Live Forever
The Tower to the Sun

With Matt Ottley
Sailing Home

The Haunted Suitcase

and other stories

Colin Thompson

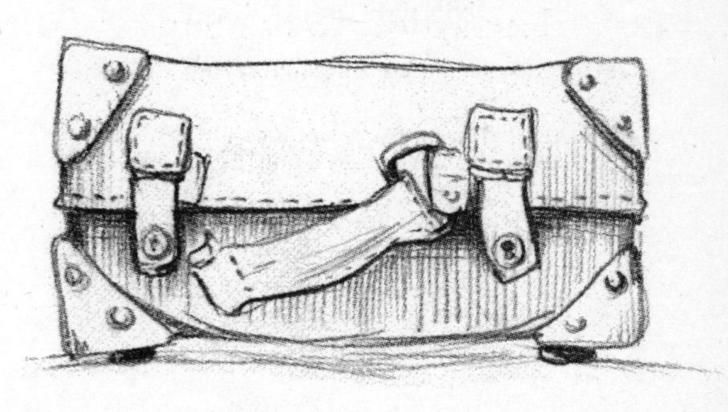

Illustrations by the author

A division of Hodder Headline plc

First published in Great Britain in 1996
by Hodder Children's Books

10 9 8 7 6 5 4 3 2 1

A Catalogue record for this book is available from the British Library

ISBN 0340 64849 X

Typeset by Phoenix Typesetting, Ilkley, West Yorkshire

Printed and bound in Great Britain by
Cox & Wyman Ltd, Reading, Berks.

Hodder Children's Books
A Division of Hodder Headline plc
338 Euston Road
London NW1 3BH

CONTENTS

For Anne who holds my hand when things get scary

The House by the Sea

In a small seaside town on the South Coast, on the edge of an ancient harbour, stood a tall dark house. It was the oldest building in the town and where it stood there had been other even older buildings before it.

Four hundred years ago the house had stood in the middle of a forest but over the centuries that had changed. One by one the trees had given way to narrow streets until now it took over an hour to walk to the countryside.

The house's antique corridors and rooms had watched as thousands of people had passed through them. Its walls had soaked up their laughter and tears, their cries and their songs so that every brick from the steep chimneys to the deepest cellar was dripping with memories and ghosts.

Over the centuries the house had seen sailing ships pass by its windows, high masts hung with soft folds of canvas and small boats with sails of gold. Then the steam boats had come and the sailing ships' time had passed. Now, the steam ships were gone too and only a few fishing boats remained.

The harbour was slowly filling with sand and rubbish so only small boats could come in and out now.

The old house had once been an inn. It had been the place where the crews of all the visiting ships had stayed. Wild men from around the world had rested and plotted in its rooms. Great parties and battles that had lasted for a week at a time had raged within the tavern walls, and in the deepest cellars, three floors below the road and out below the harbour, were rumoured to be the remains of ferocious pirates and endless tunnels into other worlds full of hidden treasure.

Every room had its ghosts and stories. Some rooms were so crowded with spirits and phantoms that at night it was impossible to hear yourself think.

There were rooms where there was so much haunting going on that the more peaceful ghosts had been forced to move out. The kitchen was like that. Things had got so bad there that the milk curdled if it wasn't put straight back in the fridge, and the smoothest gravy went all lumpy the minute the cook turned her back. On really bad days, cream of asparagus soup materialised out of thin air and flew across the room at shoulder height. And sometimes, when there was a full moon, beef-burgers in damp buns with chips and half-cooked onions appeared in the dustbin, which was the best place for them.

The family who lived in the house quite liked the ghosts. They had all grown up with them and felt as if they were part of their family and besides, some of them were very useful, particularly the Washing Up Fairy and the Manicure Elf who cleaned all the dirt out of your fingernails while you were asleep.

The two children, Peter and Alice, had known ghosts before they had even known humans. They had been visited by them before they had been born, so they took them completely for granted. They assumed that everyone had ghosts and when they heard about houses where the bath sponge didn't come when you called it, or the fried eggs always stayed on the plates and let you eat them, they thought it was very weird.

'I mean, what sort of stupid egg is that,' said Peter, 'that lets you eat it?'

The fried egg nodded and flew off through the wall.

Peter was ten and his sister Alice was eight and some of their friends were at least three hundred. And although they did take it all for granted, a few of the ghouls made Peter feel a little uneasy, especially the Plughole Fairy. Alice, on the other hand, was scared of nothing, not even the Armpit Ogre.

The house by the sea had ghosts like other houses had videos and microwaves. If there was some left-over apple pie to be heated up for lunch there was always some friendly dragon to breathe unearthly flames over it, and when everyone had finished eating, the Washing Up Fairy whisked everything up in a whirlwind and five seconds later it was back in the cupboards shining and sparkling like new.

Not everything was wonderful though. Some ghosts didn't like humans and went out of their way to be as awkward as possible. People sometimes found themselves waiting for the bathroom for hours on end while a crowd of mean spirits locked themselves inside and haunted the toilet. You could hear them splashing around and laughing, and they always left the seat up.

Things came to a head when a very important visitor was kept waiting for three hours for his breakfast, two boiled eggs with wholemeal soldiers, because the ghosts had decided to haunt every single saucepan in the house. No matter how fierce a fire the cook put a saucepan on, the ghosts turned the water to ice. In the end the visitor had cornflakes, and it wasn't until someone went out and bought an exorcise bike that the kitchen was returned to human hands.

Once this machine was installed in the cupboard under the stairs, all the ghosts and ghouls were by and large fairly well behaved.

They knew that if they pushed their luck, Alice would get on the bike and pedal furiously until they did what they were told. Those that didn't vanished in a puff of smoke and fairy dust which was then sucked up into the vacuum cleaner.

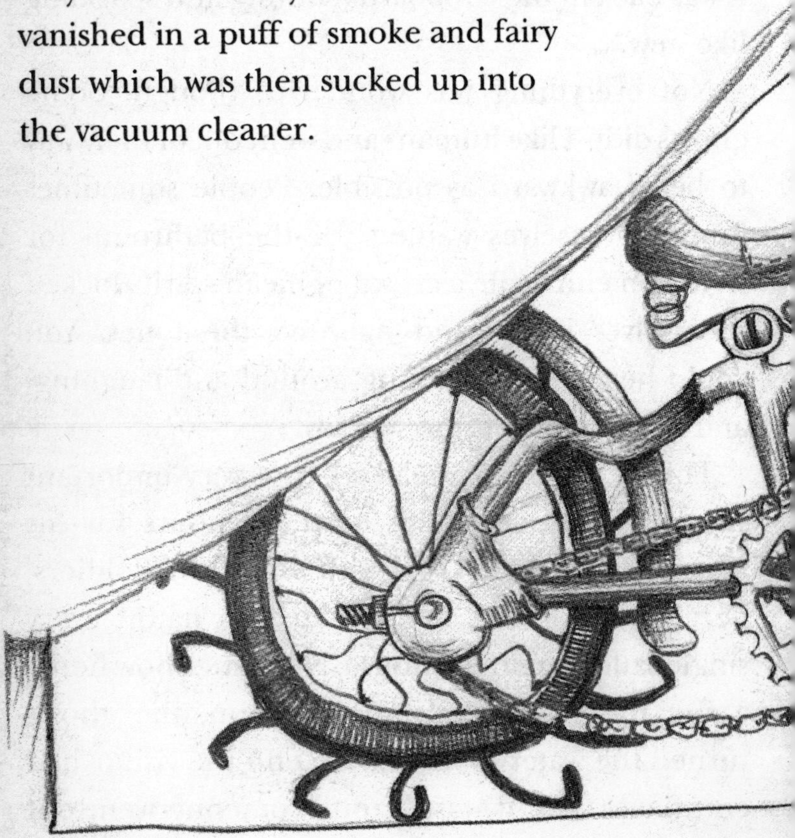

The family hardly ever talked about ghosts to people outside the house.

'We don't want people to think we're getting above ourselves,' said Peter's mother.

'I suppose they'd be jealous,' said Alice.

'Of course they would,' said Peter's granny.

There were rumours everywhere and at school the other children treated Peter and Alice with caution. Someone even said Alice was a witch, which was only slightly true. She was just a normal eight-year-old with a few pet ghosts to help her out when needed, like if she forgot her homework or couldn't remember the capital of Patagonia. Peter was a small skinny boy and was quite happy if the bigger kids kept away from him.

'Your mum flies round on a broomstick,' they shouted, which was quite untrue. If she did need to go somewhere in a hurry she went on the bus like everyone else. Of course, if it was dark and there was no–one around and she didn't have the right change for a bus ticket, *then* perhaps it was different. She did seem to get back from the supermarket very quickly sometimes, but no–one had ever actually seen her flying.

'Maybe we're ghosts ourselves,' said Peter.

'I don't think so,' said Alice. 'I don't think ghosts have spots and sticking plasters on both knees.'

Once a year, just before Christmas, a large parcel appeared inside the hall. It was enormous, much too wide to have got through the front door but it had arrived every year for as long as anyone could remember. Every year they opened it, unwrapping layer after layer, parcels inside parcels inside parcels, and every year it was the same. When they took off the last layer there was a tiny locked wooden box with a small gold key and no keyhole. They had shelves of them, hundreds of identical boxes piled up on top of each other, and jam jars full of keys.

'I reckon that one day all the keyholes will suddenly appear,' said Peter's granny, but she was wrong.

Peter's dad tried sawing one of the boxes open, but when he did it was solid wood all the way through.

'More ghost stuff,' he said.

'It'll end in tears,' said Peter's granny, but then she always said that whatever happened, and it never had.

That's how it was in the house by the sea, no–one was ever bored. New ghosts came and went, so there was always something new to talk to or run away from. In other houses people shouted and fought and got on each other's nerves. They went bald and miserable and told themselves that it was all just life. But in the house by the sea, no problem was ever still there the next morning. No-one ever lost any hair or had to go on a diet or had to clean the bath, except when the Plughole Fairy saw the full moon and was too busy. Because for all the haunting and all the rattling of chains and all the wailing, the ghosts looked after their humans. The house by the sea was their paradise and shelter where they were safe to haunt and be haunted.

DREAMS ARE GHOSTS

Dreams are ghosts of yesterday,
Of memories that are half asleep,
Of faces that have lost their names,
Of chases and forgotten games,
And things that crawl and creep.

Dreams are ghosts of yesterday,
With broken doors that won't work right,
And running scared in shoes of lead,
With groaning things beneath the bed,
That wake us screaming in the night.

Dreams are ghosts of yesterday,
Of falling helpless into space,
Of terrors that can have no words,
Of flocks of evil staring birds,
And spiders running on your face.

But dreams are ghosts of yesterday,
That let us bring back sleeping days,
When we were happy in the sun,
When we were loved by everyone,
And life was endless Saturdays.

THE HAUNTED SUITCASE

Under the roof of the house, below dark beams carved from the ribs of ancient sailing ships, was the attic. Hardly anyone ever went up there. It was a calm quiet place where the air stood still and the sounds from the rooms below were muffled by a heavy layer of dust. A thin wash of sunshine came in through a single skylight, throwing a million shadows around all the junk stored there. Boxes of books and old photographs, and chests full of ancient memories filled the place. In the darkest corners there were crumbling trunks that had stood there for hundreds of years. And in those time-worn containers, in soft paper-lined tunnels lived the most horrendous spiders you could imagine. They had been there so long that they had evolved into a unique species, a species that, because they had eaten nothing but books for hundreds of generations, had developed into a race of super-intelligent beings.

Because of the spiders, there were no ghosts in the attic. Even the most ferocious ghost was too frightened to live there. And even the most stupid ghost was not so stupid that he didn't shake with fear at the thought of them. All except one ghost, and it had no choice. Unable to move by any means, flight, telepathy or plain walking, it sat in the middle of the floor, terrified out of its tiny mind. It shone in the moonlight, a dull brown glow of antique leather. Nothing went near it, not even the dust. It was the haunted suitcase.

It was forty years since the last person had been up into the attic. The suitcase had been there then. It gave off an uneasy feeling that made people keep away from it. Sixty years before someone had put a box of old magazines up there. The suitcase had been there then too. And in 1890, when the housekeeper had been up looking for a lost maid, the suitcase had definitely been there.

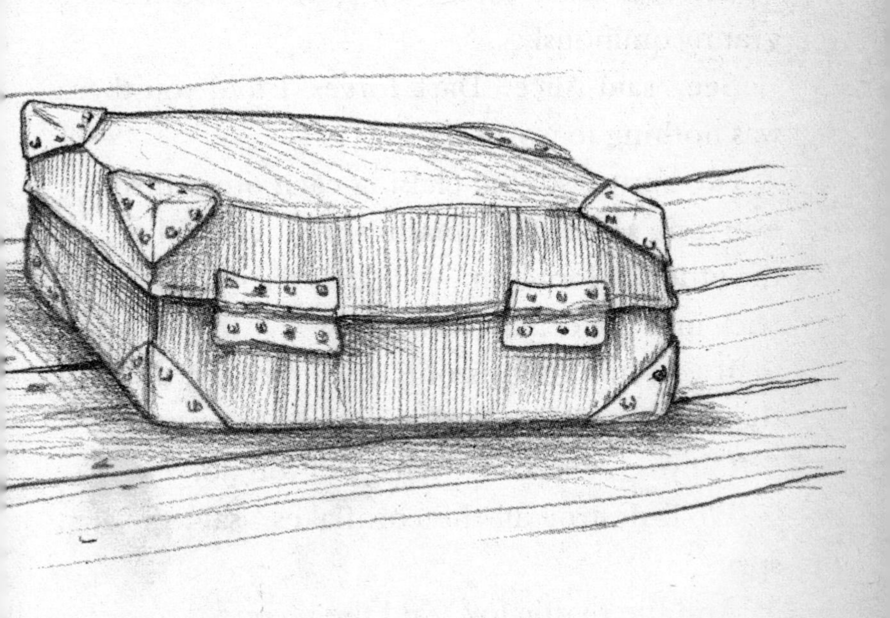

'Can we go up in the attic and play?' asked Alice one morning at breakfast.

'I suppose so,' said her mother.

'Who's *we*?' asked Peter.

'You and me,' said Alice.

'No way,' said Peter. 'I'm not going up there. It's much too dangerous.'

'Who says?' said Alice. 'I've never heard a single sound from up there.'

'Exactly,' said Peter.

'There's dark forces up there,' said Peter's granny ominously.

'See,' said Alice. 'Dark forces. I told you there was nothing to worry about.'

Two sprites started chasing each other through everyone's breakfast, splashing milk everywhere, so the attic was forgotten while they tried to get them back into the cereal box.

'If you don't let us out,' they shouted through the cardboard, 'you'll be sorry.'

'Oh yes,' said Alice. 'What will you do?'

'We'll destroy all the cornflakes,' said the first sprite.

'And the plastic toy,' said the second.

'Yeah,' said the first. 'We're cereal killers.'

By the time they'd wiped the table with the ghost of a witch's cat and finished their breakfast everyone was talking about someone else. But at lunchtime, Peter's father said, 'You know it's funny you should mention the attic. I've been thinking we should clear it out.'

'Best let sleeping dogs lie,' said Peter's granny.

'Are there dogs up there as well?' asked Alice. 'Let's go up please, please.'

'It'll end in tears,' said Peter's granny.

But after lunch they got a ladder, and Peter's father opened the trap door, climbed into the loft and disappeared.

For a long time there was complete silence. Peter and Alice stood at the bottom of the ladder looking up into the dark square in the ceiling.

'Dad,' said Alice, 'can we come up?'

'I think we should stay here and hold the ladder,' said Peter.

'You're just a big baby,' said Alice and climbed up after her father. Once again there was complete silence.

'Dad, Alice,' said Peter, 'is everything all right?'

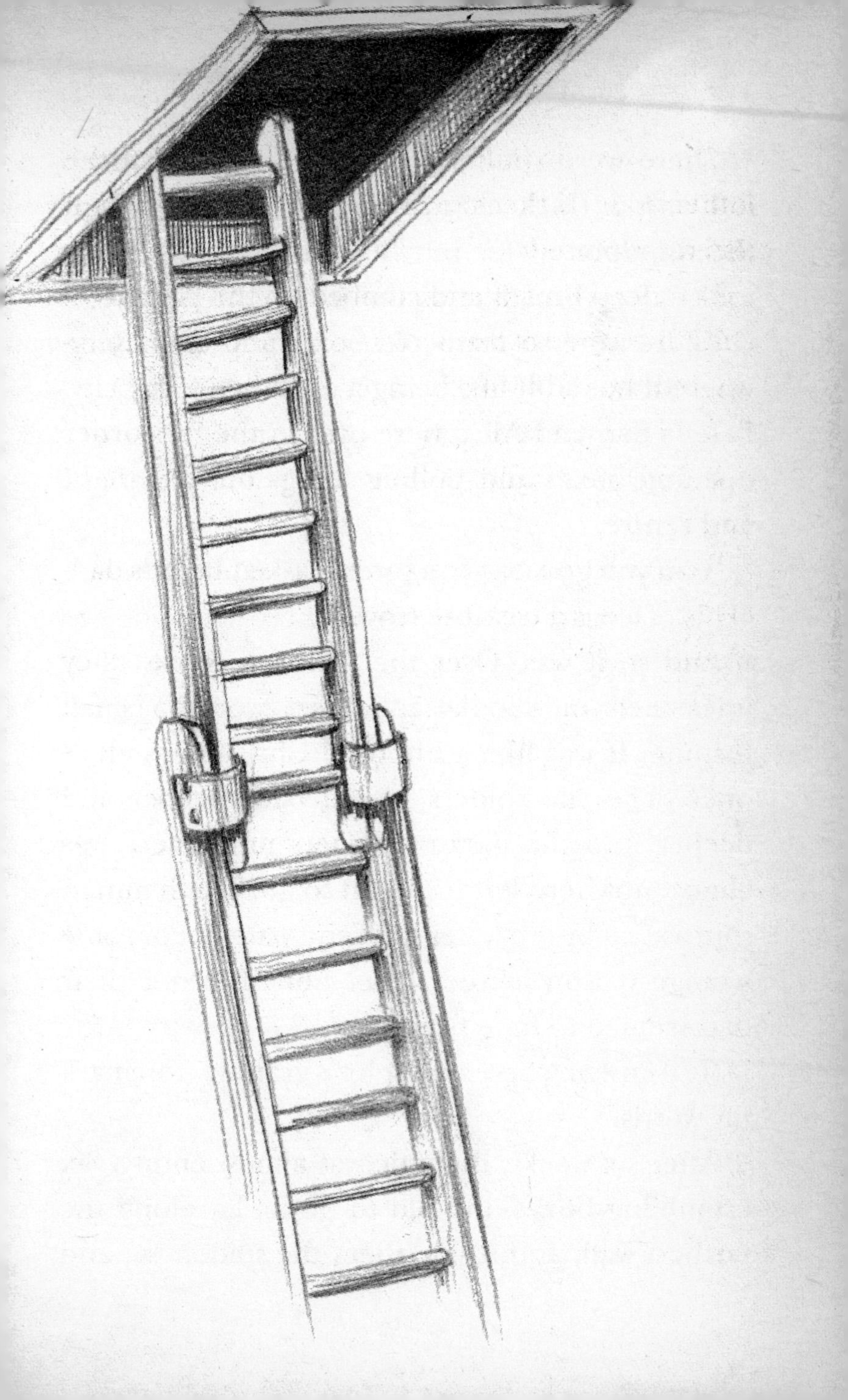

There were shuffling noises coming from the loft and a thick cloud of dust crawling out of the trapdoor. Peter put his hand over his nose, took a deep breath and climbed up the ladder.

There were so many old boxes and dust everywhere it was a bit like being a giant in a foggy city. Peter's dad and Alice were over in the far corner opening boxes and pulling things out left, right and centre.

'Can you go and get a torch?' asked Peter's dad. 'This place is a treasure trove.'

And so it was. Over the next few weeks, they unearthed old books and vases worth a small fortune. It was like a hundred Christmases all at once. The vile spiders moved back deeper and deeper into the darkest corners until there was almost nowhere left for them to go. The haunted suitcase sat by the water tank and waited. For some strange reason neither Peter nor Alice nor their dad seemed to have noticed it.

'It'll end in tears,' said Peter's granny. 'You mark my words.'

After six weeks, the attic was almost empty. Six crumbling boxes, too old to move, lay along the farthest wall, and inside them the spiders sat and waited. For the first time in three hundred years, they were frightened. It was a strange, exciting feeling but none of them knew how to handle it. Ghosts and ghouls they could deal with, but humans, especially small girls who looked like they might eat spiders, they were something different.

'Maybe we should rush out and terrorize them,' said the oldest spider, Eddie.

'Yeah,' said his sister Edna, 'If all the ghosts are scared of us, a few humans'd be easy.'

'I don't know,' said Eddie's brother, Eric. 'There are three of them.'

'Yeah,' said Eddie, 'but there are three thousand nine hundred and seventy two of us.'

'Three thousand nine hundred and seventy one,' said Edna. 'I've just eaten young Eamon.'

'I'm not sure about that girl,' said Eddie. 'She looks like she could eat all of us in one go.'

'Come on,' said Edna. 'We're the most ferocious spiders in the world.'

'Of course we are,' said Eddie. 'Let's go.'

So on the count of seven they all ran out. As they raced across the floor they suddenly heard a dreadful ear-shattering roar.

'I wonder why all spiders have names beginning with "e",' thought Edna as the roar came closer and closer. For centuries the spiders had lived in the attic. They had heard ten thousand thunderstorms and the bombs of several wars but that had all been outside. This noise was inside, right there all around them and it was the loudest thing they had ever heard.

'Oh look,' said Alice, as she vacuumed the ancient Chinese carpet that covered the attic floor, 'hundreds of tiny weeny spiders.'

They may have frightened ghosts and they may have thought they were the most ferocious spiders in the world, but because they had lived alone for so long they had forgotten that they were also some of the smallest spiders in the world, so small that Alice could hardly see them.

'Hello, tiny spiders,' she said. 'Come and play inside the vacuum cleaner.'

The last of the dust and old boxes was cleared away and it was only then that someone noticed the haunted suitcase. Peter had spent all morning cleaning and polishing and he was exhausted. He sat on the old suitcase and closed his eyes.

'Where did that come from?' said Alice.

'What?' said Peter.

'That suitcase.'

'That's odd,' said their dad. 'I wonder why we never noticed it.'

'It was probably hidden under the water tank,' said Peter. But it hadn't been. It had actually been moving slowly around the attic, hoping someone would notice it.

'I wonder what's inside,' said Alice.

They tried to open it, but the suitcase didn't want to be opened in the attic. It wanted to be downstairs in the warm sunshine. It had been cold for far too long.

'It's locked,' said Peter.

'We'll take it down to the kitchen and open it there,' said Peter's dad.

'Yeah!' thought the suitcase.

They cleared the kitchen table and put the suitcase in the middle. It wasn't very big or heavy, no bigger than a small box, really.

'Come on, come on,' said Alice, 'bash the locks off.'

As soon as the suitcase heard that, it sprung its locks and began shivering. The few ghosts that were awake ran out into the garden and Peter's granny went to the lavatory. 'I think this is where it ends in tears,' she said.

Peter lifted the lid and as he did so a few socks fell out.

'It's just full of old clothes,' he said and it was, full of socks, millions and millions and millions of them.

They poured out of the suitcase like oil from an oil well. They covered the table and piled up on the floor until everyone was ankle deep in them.

'Shut it,' shouted Peter's mum, but no–one could. They dragged the case into the garage and locked the doors and still the socks kept pouring out.

By next morning they had reached the roof and were packing themselves in tighter and tighter until the doors were straining at their hinges.

'I wish I'd taken the car out first,' said Peter's dad.

They collected up all the socks from the kitchen, three thousand and twenty seven of them. And every single one was different. Inside the haunted suitcase were all the odd socks that everyone in the world had ever lost.

'Maybe there's another suitcase somewhere with all the other ones in,' suggested Peter, but there wasn't, because the sock that got left behind was always used as a duster or a rag to clean up after a new puppy.

On Tuesday, the garage doors collapsed and the socks began to pour out into the garden. On Wednesday, Peter's Aunt Sophie, who was staying for the weekend, said she would take the suitcase. She had an idea.

She tunnelled into the garage and carried the suitcase out to a large truck. Their poor car had sock dents all over it and for months they kept finding socks in the most unlikely places. They turned up in parts of the house where the suitcase hadn't even been. The strangest one was on Christmas day when they found a very old worn out sock in the middle of the Christmas pudding.

Aunt Sophie drove the truck into the middle of a massive factory and twenty-four hours a day forever after, two hundred people sorted the socks into pairs. Because, although they were all odd socks, there are only so many different possible types of sock. So if you lost a green one with orange spots in a cottage in Scotland, someone, somewhere else in the world would, one day, be bound to lose a sock exactly the same as yours.

'It'll end in tears,' said Peter's granny, who had been put in charge of everyone in the sock factory.

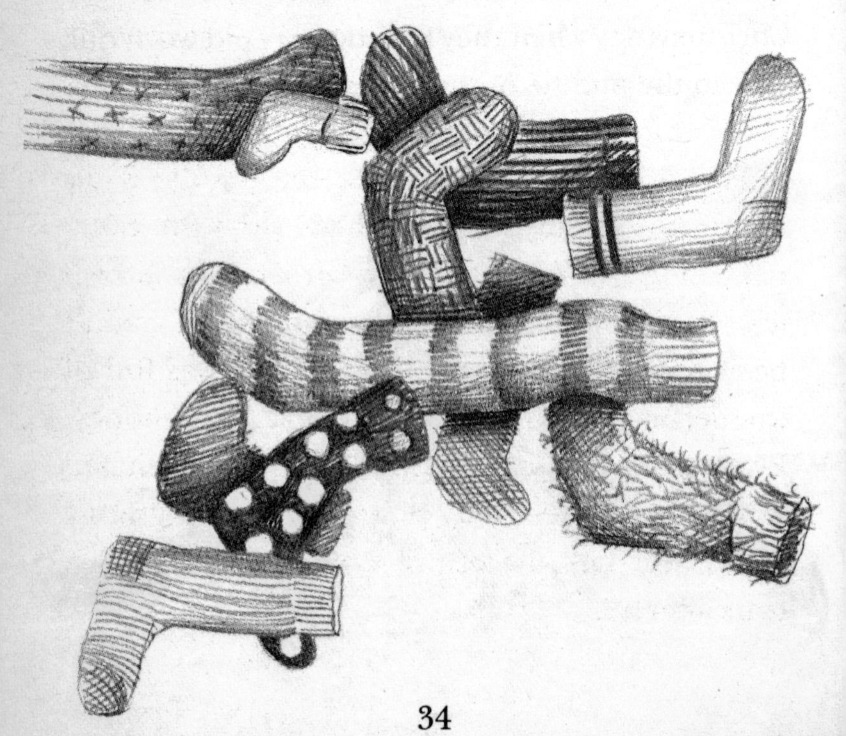

'No, no,' said Aunt Sophie. 'It'll end in pairs.'

Aunt Sophie opened a shop that just sold socks. Then she opened another one and another one until she had shops all over the world. And every day thousands of people bought new socks to replace the odd ones they had lost. Sometimes they probably bought back one of the very socks they had lost. There was even a man in Tasmania who bought his own lost socks back three times and never realised. He just thought how wonderful it was that they kept making the same pattern over and over again. And of course every day people kept on losing socks so the haunted suitcase was never empty.

The haunted suitcase sat in the middle of its huge factory, happier than it had ever been. Every day someone dusted it and stroked its brown leather skin with soft gentle polish that hadn't been tested on any animals at all and was full of wonderful things like marigolds and honey. Everyone loved the haunted suitcase because it had made them all very, very rich. Even Peter's granny finally admitted that it probably wouldn't end in tears after all.

The Curse of Dogbreath Magroo

At the back of the house up its own narrow staircase was the room of Dogbreath Magroo. It was a cold dim room known to the rest of the house as the Two-Day Room because that was the longest anyone had ever stayed there. Most people went the next morning. Some didn't even unpack their suitcases, they just turned around and left straight away.

Shadows gathered in the corners of the room, shadows that shivered and fidgeted as they tried to hide behind each other. At the one thin window was a torn grey rag, a shadow too of a once bright curtain covered in roses. The roses were echoed on the walls and like the curtain they had faded and died. The air was clammy and thick and green.

Dogbreath Magroo had been an old sea dog who lived in the room when he came back from the ocean. All his life he had travelled the oceans of the world and in every harbour and every inn the name of Dogbreath Magroo had left the same memory, a memory that could cause grown men to weep and women to faint clean away. Dogbreath Magroo had had the breath of a twenty–year–old dog that had eaten rotten cabbage leaves all his life. And this was hardly surprising because he *was* a twenty-year-old dog and he *had* eaten rotten cabbage leaves all his life.

He had lived in this room and he had died there. He had lain dead there for weeks before anyone had noticed. When something dies, after a while it begins to smell, but Dogbreath Magroo did that anyway. It was only when he stopped smelling so bad that they knew he was dead.

They had to hold auditions to find someone who could carry the old dog into the garden and bury him. Having no sense of smell just wasn't enough, for the smell of Dogbreath Magroo was so powerful you could hear it and you could feel it on your skin. At last they found someone for the job. They found someone who could sit in a bath of rancid goat yoghurt with pieces of hundred–year–old French cheese dribbling from each nostril while eating a third-hand handkerchief. They found someone with no sense of hearing, sight or smell who could feel his way into the room and fetch the old dog, someone who would do anything if the price was right.

'We should have thought of asking our accountant before,' said Peter's dad. 'It would have saved a lot of trouble.'

By the time Dogbreath Magroo was taken out of the room, his smell had left him and become a ghost. It had crept into every crack between the floorboards and behind every wrinkle in the wall-paper. It had grown and multiplied until it had taken over the whole room. The smell hid and mutated and even pretended not to be there by disguising itself as a lovely vase of flowers.

There was a never ending line of tenants willing to rent the room. It had a lovely view as the house was in a beautiful spot right on the water. The lodgers just couldn't believe how cheap it was. But it was the same every time. They dragged their suit-case bumping up the narrow staircase, hung their clothes in the wardrobe, put the framed photo of their mum on the chest of drawers and lay down for a snooze.

During the day, the ghost of Dogbreath Magroo lay still and waited. To get the full force of its powers it needed darkness. A bit of moonlight was even better. Then, while the unsuspecting visitor slept, it would do its evil. Everything in the room, even down to the mother's photograph was soon filled with the terrible smell.

And with the smell came the hair. Everything was buried under a thick layer of dog hair. Beautiful smart black suits and thick woollen sweaters were ruined for ever. The hairs were rooted deep into the clothes so no amount of brushing or cleaning could ever remove them, and whatever colour the clothes were, the hair was the opposite. The ghost could even cover the most complicated tartan with hair in six different colours. Of course, the smell was so terrible that most people didn't even notice the hair until they had packed and fled.

It was the same every time. Peter's mum had never managed to get anyone to stay in the room for more than two nights and then they had to be very drunk. They tried to remove the ghost with the exorcise bike but because it was a dog, it chased the wheels and bit the tyres.

'Something's got to be done,' she said. 'We need the money.'

'It'll end in tears,' said Peter's granny.

'We need an exorcist,' said Peter's dad, 'to drive the ghost away.'

'Well you'd better get a good one,' said Peter's granny. 'We don't want it turning up somewhere else in the house.'

There wasn't anything in the yellow pages or on the noticeboard at the sweet shop. They advertised for someone and two or three people came, but none of them were any good. They swept in wearing shiny black cloaks, velvet top hats and crept out covered in clouds of white dog hairs and confusion.

'We have to be more specific,' said Peter's mum. 'We have to say exactly what the ghost is. We need a specialist.'

'I shouldn't think there's an exorcist that just gets rid of dog ghosts,' said Peter's dad.

But there was.

A week later there was a ring at the door and a little old lady stood there. Her lumpy cardigan was done up on the wrong buttons and her tweed skirt was already covered in dog hairs.

'I've come about the advert,' she said. 'I am Gertrude Pencil and I have come to exercise the ghost of your dog.'

'Don't you mean exorcise?' said Peter's mum.

'I know what I mean,' said Gertrude Pencil.

'Can I watch?' asked Alice.

'You can get me a nice cup of tea with three sugars and a biscuit,' said Gertrude. She went into the bathroom, sat on the bed and started chanting in a strange foreign language.

'Leeh, leeh,' she wailed, then 'slurp, slurp,' as she drank her tea uttering a strange curse as her biscuit broke and fell in the cup.

All afternoon she sat cross–legged on the bed chanting. Alice sat in an old armchair and watched and at half-past four, the shape of Dogbreath Magroo appeared in the middle of the floor. It was faint at first but as the old lady reached out towards it, it became more solid and wagged its tail. The smell was terrible but the old lady didn't seem to notice.

'Leeh, leeh,' she wailed, 'leeh, leeh.'

The ghost of Dogbreath Magroo walked over to the bed and the old lady reached down and stroked it.

'Seiklaw,' she muttered and the dog followed her downstairs and out of the house never to be seen again. And only Alice knew the secret of the strange language for only she had been listening in a mirror.

The Bicyclops

On special occasions everyone had a glass of wine. If it was Christmas or someone's birthday they just got a bottle from the back of the larder; but if it was a *really* special occasion, that wine wasn't good enough. On those days they drank ancient wine from the cellar, not the cellar under the kitchen where the boiler was, or the cellars below that full of old boxes and broken furniture, but the cellars three floors down that stretched out under the harbour, cellars that only a few people knew existed and even fewer had visited.

Peter's eleventh birthday was one of the most incredible days ever. Not because Peter was eleven but because on the same day, three new Kings were crowned, there were total eclipses of the sun and the moon, and not one single person was killed on any television programme anywhere in the whole world. That day, Peter's mother decided they should have the rarest wine of all. And because it was *his* birthday, it was Peter's job to go down and get it.

He had grown up with ghosts. Since he had been a baby and the white parrot had sat on the end of his cot, he had been surrounded by them. They were as natural to him as real people and some of them had become his good friends. Nevertheless the thought of going down to the bottom cellars made Peter nervous.

'Can Alice come with me?' he asked.

'Why?' said his mother.

'Well, I might get lost,' said Peter. He didn't want to tell anyone he was frightened even though everyone knew. No–one really minded, in fact they would have been surprised if Peter hadn't been scared. It was just that no–one actually wanted to say that they would have been scared too. Peter's father had been down there a few times and he was always nervous.

'Yes, yes,' said Alice. 'I want to go.' She was a lot braver than Peter.

The first cellar was fine. It had a bright light and Peter had been down there hundreds of times. The lower cellars were all right too. The light wasn't so bright and there were lots of dark shadows, but the ghosts were all asleep and the spiders were small and timid.

The door to the third cellar was in the darkest corner and it obviously hadn't been opened for quite a long time because it was covered in cobwebs.

Peter opened the door, turned on his torch and went cautiously down the stairs. The black handrail felt warm and alive in his hand. He thought he could feel the faint and distant beat of a slowly pounding heart and it sent a cold shiver down his spine. His feet kept touching soft things that

moved in their sleep. Alice climbed down behind him singing a little song to herself.

A terrible dampness filled the air making it feel heavy and close. The grey smoothness of the walls with their even lines of cut stones gave way to jagged rocks that dripped incessantly with water and grey slime. From below, thin wisps of white smoke cut up through the air, catching the dying beams of Peter's torch. The sleepy groans of restless creatures swirled around in the invisible distance.

At last, when he thought his legs would give up if they had to go down another step, they reached the bottom and came to a small place bathed in a pool of weak yellow light. A dusty lantern hung from a hook high up in the wall. Its flame flickered and danced in the breeze blowing in from a tunnel that faded off into the darkness.

Peter started walking nervously down the tunnel, trying as hard as he could not to cry. He felt his mouth quivering and a big lump in his throat. He told himself he would never be nasty to anybody ever again if he could just get back upstairs without anything terrible happening. Dark shapes moved against a deeper darkness, or so he thought. Loud sighs tickled his imagination. He wanted to turn back but he knew he couldn't. Alice had stopped singing now, but she wasn't frightened. She was sucking a toffee.

'Do you want one?' she said, holding out a sticky brown bag.

Peter shook his head and went deeper down the tunnel. It began to get wider and the dripping water grew louder until he found himself in a mighty cave with a river running through it. Now they were way out under the sea and Peter imagined he could hear the rolling waves far above them.

His torch was completely dead now but he still held it tightly and pointed it ahead. A faint light at the far end of the cave painted the tops of the rocks with a blush of blue glaze. In the feeble glow Peter picked his way down a winding path that wove erratically through a field of stalagmites. This was the wine cellar, for around every stalagmite there were shelves full of bottles. There were thousands and thousands of bottles, reaching up into the darkness and off into the distance. There were bottles that had been there so long they were buried under dust as thick as soup.

'Which one am I supposed to get?' asked Peter.

Alice walked ahead, turned sharp left, scrambled up a rack and pulled out a bottle.

'This one,' she said.

'How do you know?' said Peter.

'Why?' said Alice.

'Why what?' said Peter.

'Why do you want to know how I know?' said Alice.

Peter had learnt a long time ago not to carry on talking to Alice when she didn't want to answer a question. Although she was only eight she could avoid answering a question all day, and if you tried to make her you usually ended up with a bad headache. Peter took a toffee and looked round for the best way back.

'This way,' said Alice, walking off in the opposite direction.

It was almost impossible to see where they were walking and in no time at all they were completely lost. The river that had been on their right was now on their left yet the distant light was still ahead of them. It was as if the rocks themselves were juggling about to confuse them. Peter tripped over something wet and furry that shambled off sideways snuffling.

'We're lost, aren't we?' he said.

'Of course not,' said Alice.

'Where are we then?' said Peter.

'We're right here,' said Alice.

Peter sat on the floor wet and cold and farther away from love and light than he had ever been before. The only good thing seemed to be that the bottle of wine hadn't broken. The darkness curled round them like a thick black nightmare and when it seemed as if things could get no worse, the ground began to shake to the pounding of gigantic footsteps. They came up the cave as a dull thunder that grew into a stomping uproar and just as they seemed to be right over them, they stopped.

Peter looked up and in front of him he saw two great big pairs of very muddy wellington boots.

Above them two pairs of equally muddy trousers led up to two grubby vests and on top of the vests were two enormous heads. Peter was terrified. The giants' arms hung down like tree trunks, and their bristly faces that hadn't been washed for months rolled from side to side. There was enough dried-up food stuck in their beards to feed five families for a fortnight. And to cap it all, in the middle of each forehead, staring wildly about but seeing nothing was one mad eye as big as a hen's egg.

'I can smell a little boy,' said the left monster.

'I smelt him first,' said the right. Peter crawled very quietly away behind a stalagmite.

'Ho, ho, ho, delicious little boy,' said the left one. 'We are the Gristle brothers, Derek and Dave, and we're going to eat you all up.'

'No we're not,' said the right one. 'We are the Gristle brothers, Dave and Derek, and we're going to cook you in a little polyunsaturated oil with a few green beans and then we're going to eat you up.'

'I don't like beans,' said Derek. 'I want chips.'

Something tapped Peter on his shoulder and he nearly jumped out of his skin. He turned round with his heart beating like a road drill. It was only Alice.

MUM

'I see you've met Derek and Dave,' she said. 'They're Cyclopses.'

'No we're not,' said Derek. 'We're Cyclopii.'

'No we're not,' sniggered Dave. 'We're Bicyclops.'

'And,' said Derek, 'we're very ferocious.'

'No we're not,' said Dave, 'we're amazingly horribly ferocious.'

'In fact,' said Derek, 'as soon as we get our spectacles on, we're going to eat you both all up.'

'No we're not,' said Dave. 'We're going to jump on you and squash you flat and then eat you all up. Hey Derek, if we eat both of them we won't need any chips or beans.'

'Well we could have some nettle salad.'

'I don't like nettles.'

'You're pathetic,' shouted Alice, hiding behind Peter just in case they weren't. 'They can't see more than a few inches in front of their faces without their glasses on and they've only got one pair between them,' she whispered.

It was true. Derek and Dave were quite incapable of seeing more than a few inches without spectacles. They were as blind as bats. Derek started poking his fingers in his brother's ear and shouting, 'Gimme the glasses, cloth–head. It's my turn.'

'Eh? No, you've got the glasses,' said Dave, mistaking a stalactite for Derek.

'No, no you've got the glasses,' insisted Derek.

'No, we're not, I've got the glasses.'

'Oh yes, so I have.'

'No we're not,' said Dave.

'Not what?' said Derek.

'Not whatever you just said.'

The terrible twins jammed their two heads tight together and tried to get a large pair of glasses across them both. When one of them got a lens lined up with his single eye the other one could no longer see anything.

'Peter'll hit you with a big stick if you come near us,' shouted Alice.

'I haven't got a big stick,' whispered Peter.

'They don't know that. They can't see,' whispered Alice.

'We might not be able to see,' said Derek, 'but we can hear. In fact we have a very keen sense of hearing.'

'Especially me,' said Dave, 'I can hear a pin drop a hundred yards away.'

'Mine's keener,' said Derek, 'I can hear a pin

drop a hundred miles away.'

'That's nothing,' countered Dave, 'I can hear a pin drop the day before it happens.'

'Well my sense of hearing's so keen, it hears things without me even asking it to.'

'Well my sense of hearing's so keen, I can hear things in photographs.'

That seemed to confuse Derek and he stood there and sulked for a bit. Then he remembered the stick and said to Peter, 'You wouldn't hit someone wearing glasses would you?'

Alice picked up a stone and threw it at them. It hit Dave on the leg and fell down inside his wellington boot.

'OWWWW, that really hurt,' he said and started to cry. 'Derek, that girl threw a great huge brick at me.'

'You big baby,' shouted Alice. 'It was just a little pebble.'

'No it wasn't, it was really enormous and sharp and pointy.'

'It can't have been very big, it's inside your welly.'

'That's my foot,' said Dave, looking confused again.

'As well as your foot, you idiot,' said Alice.

'That's Clarence, my ferret.' Clarence popped his head out of Dave's wellington boot and tried to throw the stone back at the little girl. In order to live inside Dave's welly he had to keep a clothes peg on his nose at all times. This made his eyes water, so like his owner he could hardly see what he was doing. He flung the stone in what he thought was the right direction and hit Dave on the other leg.

'OWWWWW, she's done it again,' he cried.

'Anyway,' said Alice, 'Peter's not a little boy. He's twenty feet tall and could bash you both up at once with one arm tied behind his back.'

'Derek, Derek,' wailed Dave, 'I want to go home.'

'And,' she continued, 'his favourite meal is minced cyclops on toast.' She nudged Peter, who said in as tall a voice as he could, 'Yum, yum.'

'Derek, come on, let's go home.'

'They're just pretending. He won't eat us, we're an endangered species,' said Derek. 'Anyway, we are home.'

'I need to go to the toilet,' said Dave and hurried off as fast as an almost blind one-eyed monster can. Peter realised why there were so many broken stalactites everywhere. Derek and Dave kept running into them. Without his brother for support, Derek wasn't so sure the children were bluffing and ran off after him.

'What big babies,' sneered Alice.

'I feel rather sorry for them,' said Peter. 'They seem so useless.'

'They're pathetic,' said Alice.

During all the carry-on with the two cyclops, Peter and Alice had wandered deeper into the caves and now were completely lost. It was so dark Peter could hardly see a thing, but Alice grabbed his hand and set off confidently down the path turning left and right as she went. They seemed to be going down deeper and deeper into the earth.

'How can you see where you're going?' Peter asked her.

'I eat lots of marshmallows,' said Alice. 'They make you see in the dark.'

'I thought it was carrots that did that,' said Peter.

'Well, I don't like carrots. I like marshmallows,' said Alice as if that explained everything.

A deep humming came from far above them and the rocks felt warm under their feet.

'What's that noise?' asked Peter.

'It's just a submarine,' said Alice.

'Oh yes,' said Peter, 'and I suppose the warmth is the earth's core?'

'That's right.'

'Come on,' said Peter. 'You'll be telling me the Lost City Of The Dinosaurs is just round the corner.'

'Don't be stupid,' said Alice. 'We should have

turned left back there for that. This is the way to the lifts.'

'Lifts?' said Peter.

'Well you don't suppose we're walking all the way back up hundreds of stairs do you?' said Alice. 'We're hundreds of feet below the house.'

It was another of those times when talking to Alice would give you a bad headache. Peter said nothing and followed his little sister through the darkness. At last the rough path grew smooth and flat and they could see a light ahead. The rocks changed into smooth walls and there in front of them were the lift doors. Alice pressed the button and far in the distance wheels began to turn. Suddenly a great roaring and commotion came down the tunnel behind them.

It was Derek and Dave. They charged down the path, crashing and falling over each other. In the bright light they looked sad and pathetic. Their elbows and knees were covered in sticking plasters. Their hair was uncombed and knotted and their clothes were filthy.

'Can we come with you?' asked Derek.

'We won't eat you, honest,' said Dave.

'Why?' said Alice.

'We're lonely,' said Derek. 'There's only dinosaurs to talk to and they've only got brains as big as walnuts.'

'And they think *we're* stupid,' said Dave.

'We don't want to be giants anymore,' said Derek. 'We want to be something nice.'

'But you *are* giants,' said Peter. 'How can you be something else?'

'Don't listen to him,' said Alice. 'He's as dumb as a dinosaur.'

Derek and Dave nudged each other and giggled. It sounded a bit like two huge trucks running out of diesel.

'What would you like to be?' asked Alice.

'Garden gnomes,' said Derek.

'With fishing rods,' said Dave.

'Or maybe a bird bath,' said Derek.

'OK,' said Alice. 'I'll go and get the fairies at the bottom of the garden to come and change you.'

'You will come back, won't you?' asked Dave.

'Yes,' said Alice, 'but you have to promise not to try and eat the fairies or they'll change you into traffic cones.'

'We promise,' said Derek.

'Hold on, hold on,' said Dave. 'What's a traffic cone?'

When Alice told him, he thought it sounded pretty good.

'Maybe I'd rather be one of them,' he said, but Derek told him to shut up and before they could start arguing again the lift came and Peter and Alice got in.

An hour later Alice returned with the fairies from the bottom of the garden. They chucked a bit of fairy dust on Derek and Dave's wellies, chanted a few strange words and waved their wands. There was a big puff of smoke and the two giants changed into gnomes. In the back garden of the house by the sea there were twenty–seven gnomes, four birdbaths and a barbeque which had all been ogres at one time or another. Now and then one of them got bored and missed all the shouting and roaring, so fairies from the bottom of the garden just changed them back again, but usually the gnomes spent the rest of their lives standing happily by the garden pond waiting for the big fish.

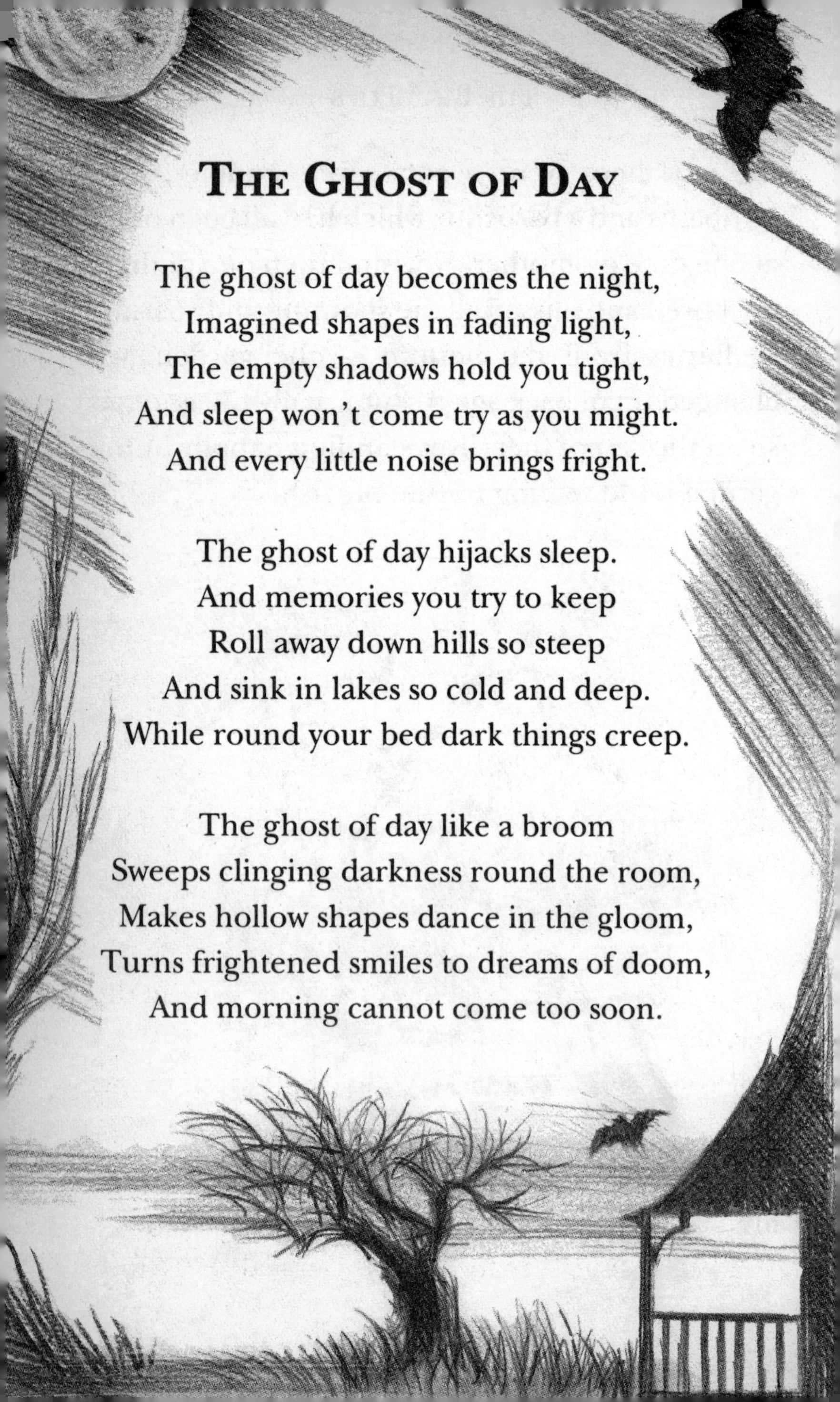

The Ghost of Day

The ghost of day becomes the night,
Imagined shapes in fading light,
The empty shadows hold you tight,
And sleep won't come try as you might.
And every little noise brings fright.

The ghost of day hijacks sleep.
And memories you try to keep
Roll away down hills so steep
And sink in lakes so cold and deep.
While round your bed dark things creep.

The ghost of day like a broom
Sweeps clinging darkness round the room,
Makes hollow shapes dance in the gloom,
Turns frightened smiles to dreams of doom,
And morning cannot come too soon.

George's Revenge

George the budgerigar was depressed. Everyone in the whole world was having a better time than he was. The old rat under the sink was having more fun than he was. Even the fleas in the rat's ears had more fun than him. Even the blind slugs in the deepest cellars who had nothing to eat but really old slime and who kept getting trodden on by blind giants, had a more fulfilling life than he did. His cage was in the dampest darkest corner of the kitchen and it had been put there deliberately. No-one talked to him anymore except to tell him to shut up when he told them all what a pretty boy he was.

'If I just dropped dead right now,' he said, 'no-one would care. They'd just stick me in an old carrier bag with the dog's hair and chuck me in the dustbin.'

'Don't be so pathetic,' said the ghost in his mirror.

'Or they'd chuck me on the compost heap,' he moaned, 'and bury me under the potato peelings.'

'I can't stand any more of this,' said the ghost.

'I'm off to haunt the shaving mirror in the bathroom.'

'That's it,' said George, 'go off and leave me. Everyone else has.'

George the budgerigar was depressed and the more he sat and sulked, the angrier he got. He swore under his breath, crashed up and down his perch and kicked lumps out of his cuttlefish. He was furious and there is nothing more dangerous in the whole world than an angry budgerigar. At least that's what George told himself.

'They'll be sorry,' he muttered. 'They'll wish they'd been nicer to me, by the time I'm finished with them.'

'Oh yeah,' said the spider that lived in the top of his cage, 'what are you going to do, spill your millet on the floor?'

'I'll show them,' said George. He knew there wasn't really anything he could do but he was so furious he wasn't thinking clearly. It was midnight and everyone had gone off to bed leaving the light on.

'They probably did it deliberately,' said George, 'just to keep me awake all night.'

He glared at the light with all the anger his little

body could muster. The dirty yellow globe was a symbol of everything horrible that had ever been done to him. It was a mean pale copy of the sun but it gave him no warmth. He narrowed his eyes and stared right into the lightbulb and then something wonderful happened. The lightbulb exploded.

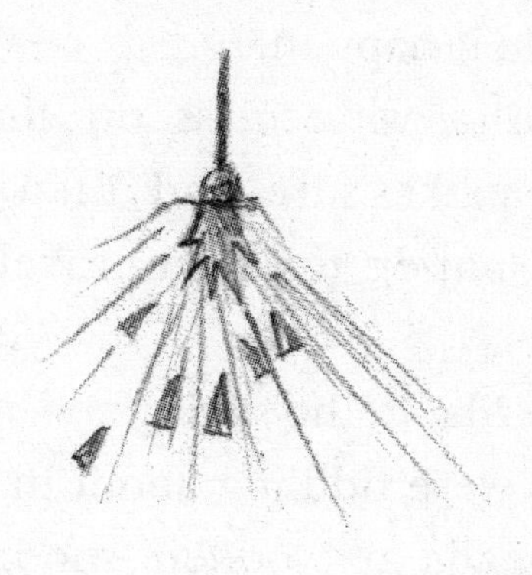

'Wow, telekinesis,' he thought, but as he fell asleep in the peaceful darkness he thought it was probably just a coincidence.

As the sun crept in through the curtains the next morning, George looked at its light glinting in all the pieces of broken glass on the kitchen table and he knew it hadn't just been an accident. He knew he'd made it happen.

He shattered a wine glass on the draining board just to make sure and then made the whole roll of paper towels unravel onto the floor.

'This is more like it,' he said.

A few ghosts were fiddling about in the corner and George made a wooden spoon fly right through them. They flew behind the bread bin and peered out into the apparently empty room.

'No more mister nice guy,' said George. 'From now on I'm the king of the kitchen.' And he opened and closed his cage door a few times to prove it.

He could have escaped, flown right away to freedom, the window was wide open enough; but no, it was going to be more fun staying where he was.

Before he took on the world, he had to develop his powers. He tried to open the oven but it was too heavy and he managed to turn on the cold tap but the hot one was turned off too tightly. It would take practice and self–discipline until he realised his full potential. And, as proud as he was of his new powers, he would have to make sure he didn't tell anyone, not even his best friend.

Not even my best friend, he thought. I haven't got a best friend, he realised, getting angry again. I haven't even got a worst friend.

He had to break the rest of the wine glasses and pull all the petals off a vase of flowers to cheer himself up.

When the family came down for breakfast and found all the mess, they just assumed it was the ghosts. As they cleaned up the mess George taunted them by telling them what a pretty boy he was but they just told him to shut up.

'Shut up is it?' he said to himself. 'I'll give them shut up.' And he turned off the fridge. By lunchtime someone noticed water leaking out of the door and the family spent all afternoon shouting at each other.

'It'll end in tears,' said Peter's granny and for

once she was right. Peter and Alice, neither of whom could actually reach the switch, were both blamed for it. After all, who else could have done it?

'It must have been the ghosts,' said Peter, but all the ghosts denied it.

'You always believe the ghosts,' said Alice to their parents. 'It *must* have been one of them.'

George felt a bit sorry for the children but it only lasted a hundredth of a second. It was them who had put him in the dark corner and it was them who always forgot to clean out the bottom of his cage. And thinking of the bottom of his cage gave him an idea, all those horrible wet seed husks and tiny black and white droppings.

'Well, well,' he thought, 'it looks like muesli, just like it.'

That night it took George over an hour to get the lid off the muesli container and another two hours to make everything fly out of the bottom of his cage and drop into the jar. After that it took an hour to mix it all up and spread a thin layer of oats and raisins on the top, and finally another hour to get the lid back on. It was almost dawn by the time he had finished and he was exhausted, but it had been worth it. He broke the new lightbulb and then fell asleep into a wonderful dream where he was back in Australia flying through the trees with thousands of his relations.

Of course the ghosts got the blame for the muesli and the second lightbulb, and when they told the humans it had been George no–one believed them.

'Come on,' said Peter's mum. 'Look at him, he's just a stupid budgie.'

George jumped up and down and pecked his mirror and looked as dim as he could.

'Who's a pretty boy? Who's a pretty boy?' he said, and pretended to fall off his perch.

'See,' said Peter's dad. 'He can't even sit on his perch without tripping over his feet.'

Morons, thought George.

After a week of breaking lightbulbs and chucking food around, George decided it was time for bigger and better things. He was fed up with spilling people's tea and reckoned it was time to leave his familiar cage, time to come out and play. As soon as everyone was asleep he opened his cage door and flew into the hall. It was a full moon and everywhere was lit up with a cool blue light. Outside, the town was silent apart from the distant sound of a few early morning cars.

Outside, thought George, maybe I should fly away! But it wasn't time to chase freedom, it was time for revenge.

Upstairs he could hear Peter's granny snoring. It sounded like an old lion with a bad cold. George flew into the lounge and turned on the television and the radio and the hi-fi, and the radio in the kitchen and the television in Peter's room and the television in Alice's room and the alarm clock beside Peter's parents' beds. Peter's dad was in the shower before he realised it was still dark outside. Peter's mum was on her way downstairs to let the dog out before she realised it was only two o'clock in the morning.

'This is great,' said George, shutting off the hot

tap and catching Peter's dad with a sudden blast of icy cold water.

Every night George thought up more nasty tricks to play on the family who had treated him so badly.

'I'll teach them not to love me,' he said. 'I'm a pretty boy. Who's a pretty boy? Me!'

And every morning it was the ghosts who got the blame. By now the ghosts knew it was George causing all the havoc, but of course no–one would believe them.

'He's just a stupid budgie,' insisted Peter's mum.

George jumped up and down and pecked his mirror.

'Who's a pretty boy? Who's a pretty boy?' he said and was laughing so much he really did fall off his perch.

'See,' said Peter's dad. 'He can't even sit on his perch without tripping over his feet.'

This is brilliant, thought George.

'Look, we know it's one of you ghosts,' said Peter's mum, 'and if you don't stop it, we'll get the exorcise bike out and get rid of the lot of you.'

That night the ghosts had a meeting.

'We've got to do something about this wretched bird or we'll all be homeless,' said Elvira, Queen of the Witches.

'The trouble is,' said the Toothbrush Fairy, 'he's not frightened of any of us.'

'What we have to do,' said Bert the Ghoul of the Breadbin, 'is make the humans catch him at it.'

The curtains flew open. Something fluttered across the window and a squeaky voice asked them who was a pretty boy.

'Damn,' said Elvira, 'that miserable bird's been listening to every word we've said.'

George made a CD fly across the room and slot into the hi-fi. It was a Welsh male voice choir and as it blared out through the house, the ghosts fled in terror. The budgie flew after them taunting loudly.

'Who's a pretty clever boy? Who's a pretty clever boy?' he shouted.

The music had woken up Nigel the old dog, and he was blundering around the kitchen banging into the furniture.

'Stupid animal,' thought George and tipped a jar of honey over him. Nigel spent the rest of the night licking his coat until all the honey was inside him, apart from the nice even layer on Peter's bed and clothes and carpet and wallpaper.

For two weeks George flew round the house every night creating chaos. The ghosts persuaded Peter's mum to lock the kitchen door and take away the key but George just concentrated hard until the lock opened. Just for good measure, he took the door off and made the hinges fly down the garden into the harbour.

After a fortnight, George began to get bored. There were only so many lightbulbs you could explode, only so many times you could wake everyone up before it stopped being fun.

Maybe it's time to go outside, he thought.

He lifted the letterbox and looked out into the night. It was cold outside, too cold for a small bird that should have been living in Australia, but a voice inside him told him to fly away. So he did.

'Got him,' said Elvira, Queen of the Witches as she tied up the letterbox with more string than even the most telepathic budgie could undo.

'By the time he gets half that lot undone, he'll have frozen to death,' she said.

'Serves him right,' said the Toothbrush Fairy.

'Yes, but then he'll be a ghost,' said Ensor the Demon of the Drains, 'and he'll come and live with us.'

'Damn,' said Elvira, 'I hadn't thought of that,' and they spent the next twenty minutes undoing all the string and swearing at each other.

'What are we going to do?' said the Toothbrush Fairy.

'We'll talk to Alice,' said Elvira. 'She'll believe us and she'll think of something.'

'She won't believe us, no-one does,' said Ensor.

But she did and she was a wise child and had been wondering why George, who had been such a chirpy bird, had suddenly become so angry.

'Ask him what he's so cross about,' said Alice.

'I don't speak budgerigar,' said Elvira. 'None of us do.'

So Alice took George's cage down from the dark corner in the kitchen and put it on the table by the window in her bedroom. She cleaned everything and gave George a new piece of cuttlefish and a red plastic mirror.

'This is more like it,' he thought.

Alice brought him fresh fruit every day and taught him all the rude words she knew. George had never been so happy.

'Who's a pretty boy?' he said to his reflection.

'Who's a pretty boy?' said the reflection.

'Both of us,' said George.

'Both of us,' said the reflection.

And both of them lived happily ever after, because all George had ever really wanted was someone to talk to, and a nice bit of cuttlefish, and a nice seat by the window.

The Moth who Couldn't Haunt

To be successful as a ghost you need to be quite big. Probably the smallest you could be and still really frighten someone would be the size of a spaniel. Though if you were a rat you would probably manage to scare anyone whether you were a ghost or not.

Alan the moth knew this. He knew that ghost moths were not going to frighten anyone.

'What is the point of it all?' he said. 'If I can't frighten anyone, why did I become a ghost?'

'Well, you're probably the *only* ghost moth there's ever been,' said Nigel the dog.

Alan had landed on Nigel's left foot and as the dog was the sort of dog who would talk to anyone, they had started chatting.

'I probably am,' said Alan. 'I mean the idea of a ghost moth is just so stupid, who'd want to be one?'

'You must be able to frighten someone,' said Nigel.

'No,' said Alan, 'not a sausage.'

'Well, no, I wouldn't expect you to be able to

frighten a sausage,' said Nigel. 'Mind you, it's not difficult. I can frighten sausages.'

'It's an expression,' sighed Alan. 'It doesn't *really* mean frightening sausages.'

Nigel was lying out on the back porch in the warm summer evening. A crowd of moths who weren't dead were bashing their heads against a lightbulb above him.

'At least I don't get headaches any more,' said Alan. 'Not like that lot up there.'

'Maybe you could go and haunt them,' said Nigel.

'It's worth a try,' agreed Alan. He flew up to the light and flitted round the moths. They were so busy crashing into the bulb that they didn't even notice him. When he flew through the glass and flapped around inside the bulb they just got jealous and chased him away.

'Maybe you're starting too big,' said Nigel. 'Maybe you should try and haunt some ants.'

'Good idea,' said Alan. 'What's an ant?'

'Little tiny black things that live in nests in the ground,' said Nigel.

'With all those wiggly legs,' said Alan, 'the things that eat sugar and keep getting in the biscuits?'

'Yes.'

'Er no,' said Alan. 'I can't haunt them.'

'Why not?' asked Nigel.

'I'm frightened of them,' said Alan. 'Nasty wriggly things, they get all over you and squirt acid on your legs.'

'What about fleas?' said Nigel.

'They don't keep still long enough,' said Alan.

'Well I can't think of anything else,' said Nigel. He was fed up with Alan. He had a really ripe bone buried down the garden and he went off to look for it.

'It should be all sticky and maggoty by now,' he thought, and he drooled in anticipation.

Alan fluttered through the house but it was the same everywhere. No–one took any notice of him at all. It was rubbish being a ghost.

'I wish I was dead,' he thought. And when he realised he already was he got *really* depressed.

'I wish I was nothing,' he said. Which he was, really. He was no more than the sort of thing you think you catch a glimpse of in the corner of the eye, and when you look round there's nothing there.

'If I was fifty million times better than I am now, I could be pathetic,' he thought.

He flew into the bathroom. The street light shone through the frosted glass filling the room with a pale yellow light and as he flew round and round *he* caught a glimpse of something in the corner of *his* eye. Every time he turned it was gone, but he knew there was something there. He could almost see it. He flew faster and faster determined to catch it up. If he hadn't been a ghost the blood would have been rushing to his head.

Suddenly there it was, a shimmering terrifying thing flying straight at him. It had piercing eyes and pale yellow wings that flashed so fast they were a blur. There should have been a roar in the air but instead there was an eerie silence. Alan was scared out of his wits and tried to get away, but the vision was racing towards him.

And then he saw what it was. Flying straight towards him, staring right into his eyes was a ghost. Closer and closer it came and then as Alan flew through the mirror it disappeared and he realised what had happened.

At last Alan the moth had managed to haunt someone. He had haunted Alan the moth and scared himself out of his wits.

THE CREATURE FROM THE BLACK DUSTBIN

On Friday nights they always had beefburgers for tea. It had been like that for as long as Peter could remember. Four for his father, three each for his mother and him, and two each for Alice and the dog, Nigel. Then one Friday, quite out of the blue, Peter's mother said:

'We're not eating meat anymore,' and she put a large pan of strange looking stew on the table. There were lots of beans drowning in it and lumps of purple vegetables which she said were the healthiest thing in the whole world.

Peter's dad looked depressed but said nothing. Peter didn't know what to say, and Alice ate three bowlfuls. Nigel sulked under the table. One lick had told him that whatever his mistress had put in his bowl, it certainly wasn't food.

Peter and his dad picked around their plates until Peter's mother went off to the kitchen.

'Here, quick, get rid of all this purple stuff,' said Peter's dad.

Peter was about to wrap it up in a piece of paper

when his mother came back with a weird looking cake. He spent the rest of the meal with a very wet pocket.

'Slice of Wholemeal Banana and Turnip cake, anybody?' she said, brightly. Peter's dad went down to the pub where he spent the evening drinking beer and eating pickled eggs. Peter squirmed around in his sticky trousers and Alice ate four slices. Nigel carried his piece of cake out into the garden and dropped it on a fly.

'I'm going to fade away and die,' he thought, pushing the cake to one side and eating the fly. Next door's dribbly cat came over the fence, and the miserable dog cheered himself up by chasing it up the apple tree. Later on Alice came out and ate Nigel's piece of cake and forty–eight dog hairs.

Up in his room Peter screwed up his face, put his hand into his pocket and pulled out the purple mess. It felt all warm and slimy like some deep sea creature from the black lagoon. He put it in a plastic box and hid it under the bed behind his comics. He looked at the calendar. It was Friday the thirteenth.

While his mother was scraping the stew off Alice and putting her to bed, Peter slipped down to the corner shop and stocked up on smokey–bacon crisps and chocolate.

Over the next few weeks the plastic box under Peter's bed slowly filled up. The original purple stuff sat in the corner growing a green fur coat and was joined by a whole variety of things as Peter's mother produced more and more amazing meals. There were huge red beans that felt like slugs and little hard white things that looked like tiny eyes. They began to get beefburgers again but now they tasted as if they were knitted out of grass. Even the bread looked grubby.

'Mum,' asked Alice, 'why's the bread all brown?'

'It's much better for you,' said her mother.

'I like clean bread better,' said the little girl, and then ate half a loaf with the colour completely hidden under a mountain of strawberry jam.

Nigel the dog was all right. Peter's dad suddenly started taking him for a walk every night and the two of them always came back smelling of vinegar and warm chips. On Wednesdays when Peter's mum went to her yoga classes, Peter's dad brought chips back for Peter and they had to hide the greasy paper in the bottom of the dustbin before she got back.

After a while the food under Peter's bed began to smell. At first Peter pretended it was his socks but when the two ogres who lived in his slippers refused to go to sleep, Peter knew he had to get rid of it. He got down on his knees and reached under the bed for the box. As his fingers touched it he thought he felt it pull away.

'It's probably just my imagination,' he said.

He pulled the box out and when his mother went out to the shops he took it down to the dustbin.

'That's funny,' he thought, as he carried it downstairs, 'it still feels warm.'

That night he realised how dumb he'd been. He'd just dropped the box into the dustbin and the next time his mother threw something away, she'd see it. He wasn't too happy creeping round the house at night. Most of the ghosts knew him and most of them were friendly but there were some who only came out on the full moon who were less friendly. And tonight was a full moon.

Peter persuaded the two ogres who lived in his slippers to go with him and he tiptoed downstairs and out into the back yard. It was all pretty quiet except when he went through the kitchen and the lightbulb exploded. The back yard was glowing in the strange blue light of the moon and something felt not quite right.

'Well, we're going back to bed,' said the slipper ogres and vanished back into the house.

Peter lifted the dustbin lid and there was the box, but it was open and it was empty. The lid was split from side to side and the inside of the box was perfectly clean.

'Something must have eaten it,' thought Peter, but in the dark shadows at the bottom of the garden a pair of purple eyes were watching him. He pushed the container under some rubbish and went back into the house.

After that, things started to go missing from the back garden. Not the sort of things that someone might come in to steal, but odd things. First all the perfume disappeared out of the roses and the earth vanished out of the flowerbeds. One morning all the green mould on the patio had gone.

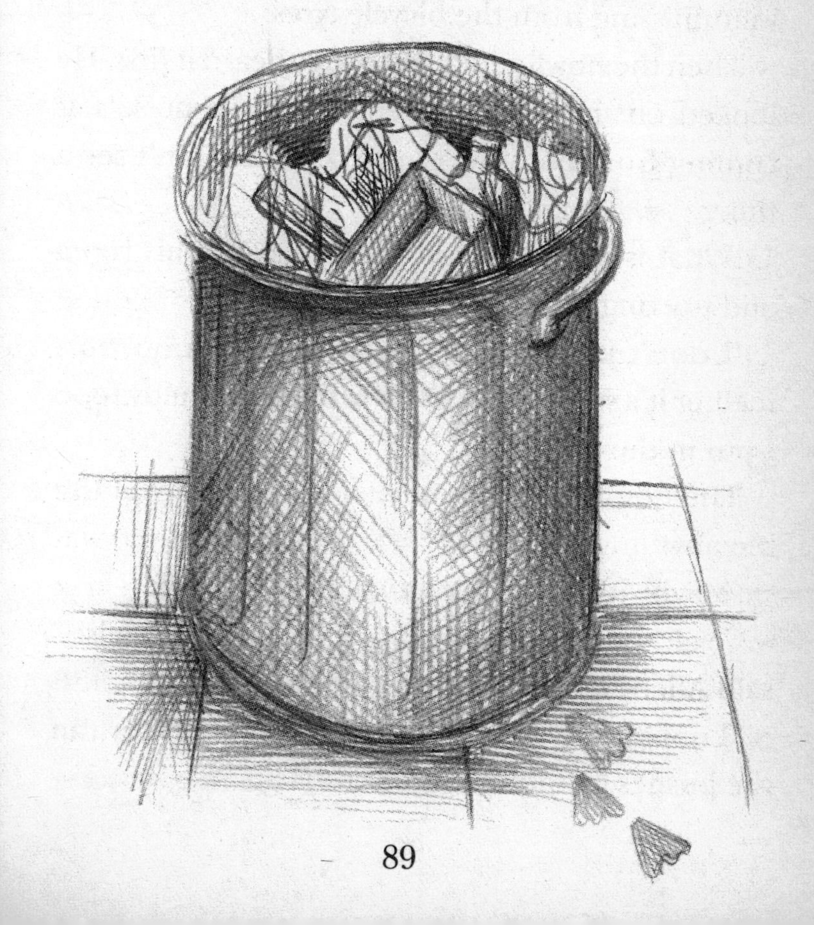

'It can't be the ghosts,' said Peter's mum. 'They move things about, but they don't steal things.'

'It's not kids,' said Peter's dad. 'They couldn't take the smell out of the flowers.'

'It'll end in tears,' said Peter's granny. She was annoyed because she'd left her best boots in the garden and the next morning all the polish had been taken off them. On the same night the air went missing from the bicycle tyres.

Then the howling started. Peter heard it first. He looked out into the garden where the noise was coming from but it was so dark, he couldn't see a thing.

'What is it?' asked Alice, coming into his room and peering out of the window.

'I don't know,' said Peter, 'but I've a horrible feeling it's something to do with that mouldy food I put in the dustbin.'

The howling grew louder but they still couldn't see anything.

'Maybe it's throwing its voice,' said Peter.

'Well, I wish it would throw it somewhere else,' said Alice, 'and stop waking us up.'

'Look, there's something there,' said Peter, 'in the bushes by the shed.'

'Purple eyes,' said Alice.

As they watched, the eyes moved out into the middle of the lawn. All they could see was a dark shape. The creature seemed to have no arms or legs, no ears or tail. It was just a vague fuzzy shape.

'I think it's a being from another dimension,' said Alice.

'What makes you say that?' said Peter.

'I don't know,' said Alice. 'It looks like it's hovering above the ground. Let's go down and have a look.'

'I don't think I want to go near it,' said Peter, but Alice was already on her way downstairs. They looked through the kitchen window. The creature was still there, sitting on the lawn eating celery.

'Come on,' said Alice, and she opened the back door.

The creature ran off into the bushes but the two children could still see its purple eyes glowing in the dark.

'It's all right,' said Alice. 'We won't hurt you.'

'Promise?' said the creature.

'Who are you?' demanded Peter. 'What are you doing here?'

'I am Pesto,' said the creature, coming out into

the moonlight. 'I am a being from another dimension.'

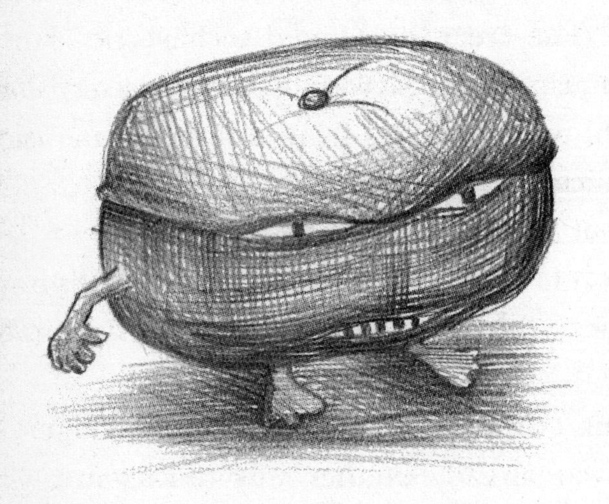

'What are you doing here?' said Alice. 'What do you want?'

'I have been sent here from my planet to eat up all the lonely and unwanted vegetables,' said Pesto. 'We got a message from some carrots that were trapped under your bed.'

'Was it you who took the stuff out of the dustbin?' said Peter.

'Yes,' said Pesto. 'The trouble is that I'm stuck here. I don't seem to be able to get back to my planet.'

'Didn't they tell you how to get back?' said Peter. 'Didn't they give you a spaceship?'

'Er, no, they just put me in a big paper bag,' said Pesto, 'and the next thing I knew I was here.'

'Are you sure you're from another dimension?' asked Alice. 'Because I keep thinking I've seen you somewhere before.'

'You can't have done,' said Pesto, 'I come from another solar system billions of light years away.'

'I don't care,' said Alice. 'I know I've seen you somewhere before.'

In a rage Pesto ran into the bushes and began to howl. He flashed his purple eyes but no–one was scared. In fact, Nigel the dog went over and lifted his leg on the creature, and then the howling stopped.

'I know where I've seen you,' said Alice. 'You're the thing my granny puts her feet on when she's watching television.'

Peter went into the bushes and dragged the screaming creature out onto the lawn where Alice sat on it, carefully avoiding Nigel's wet bit.

'You're just a stupid cushion,' said Alice.

'No I'm not. I am Pesto the creature from the black dustbin. I am a being from another dimension. The cushion effect is just a disguise,' said the cushion.

'You feel like a cushion to me,' said Alice and she dragged it inside to its place by her granny's chair.

'Now you stay there,' said Alice, 'and if we see you so much as wrinkle your corduroy, we'll pull your stuffing out.'

The cushion started to shake. Its corners hunched up like shoulders and tears poured out of its purple eyes.

'I'm *not* a cushion,' it insisted. 'I am a being from another dimension and I want to go home.'

'Well, go on then,' said Alice.

'I've told you,' said the cushion creature. 'I don't know how to.'

'We'll help you,' said Peter. Now the creature was crying he felt quite sorry for it. 'We'll go and ask the ghosts and see if they can think of anything.'

Alice was about to say that she didn't believe any of it, that she knew that the thing was her granny's cushion. But then she saw something in the shadows by the couch. It was her granny's cushion. She dragged it out and stuck it down beside Pesto.

'Gladys,' said Pesto. 'Is that you?'

'Oh, Pesto,' said Peter's granny's cushion. 'You've come for me, after all these years.'

'What?' said Peter.

'Oh no,' said Alice. 'I don't believe it.'

But it was true. Pesto really was a creature from the far side of space and Peter's granny's cushion was his long lost sweetheart who had been sent to earth twenty years before to rescue some unhappy radishes.

'I've been so lonely,' said Gladys. 'Twenty years of watching soaps on television every day. I nearly went mad.'

'I missed you so much,' said Pesto, nuzzling up to the threadbare old cushion. 'I'd almost forgotten how beautiful you were.'

Pesto forgot all about going home. He and Gladys sat side by side in front of the couch and in the afternoons they watched the soaps together. They had both been lonely for so long but now they were together again. Now they would live happily ever after.

The Plughole Fairy

The old house by the sea was famous for having the oldest bathroom in the country. While everyone else had been sitting in tin baths by the kitchen fire or standing out in the rain to get a wash or just being very dirty, the people in the house by the sea sat in comfort in a great big marble bathtub that had been brought from China.

It stood on four gold lion's feet in the middle of the bathroom. Huge brass taps on heavy pipes grew out of the floor and in a basket on the side of the bath a family of antique sponges sat and quivered.

There was something vaguely uncomfortable about having a bath in the ancient tub. It wasn't that the sponges tried to pull away when you picked them up and all the time you were using them, they wriggled in your fingers. And it wasn't that being stuck in the middle of the blue-painted room, you felt as if you were in a boat out at sea. Nor was it that the soap had a terrible habit of slipping under the water and popping up in embarrassing places. It was the thought of the Plughole Fairy.

No-one had actually seen the Plughole Fairy but

they all knew it was there.

'Everybody knows about the Plughole Fairy,' said Alice. 'It hides down the plughole and sucks the water out of the bath and if you stay in the bath too long, it blows the plug up in the air and pulls your toes down the drain.'

'No, it doesn't,' said Peter, 'those are just silly stories.'

'Well what's all that gurgling noise when the water runs away then?' asked Alice.

'It's just the water,' said Peter.

'Water can't make a noise,' said Alice. 'It's just wet stuff, it hasn't got a mouth.'

'Rivers have,' said Peter.

'Well I've got a picture of the Fairy, so there,' said Alice.

'Show me,' said Peter. Alice pulled a piece of folded paper out of her pocket and said, 'This is it, but you'd better not look at it or you'll go crazy mad with fright.'

'Have *you* looked at it?' Peter asked.

'Of course not, I'm not stupid,' said his sister.

'Well *I'm* not frightened of a picture,' said Peter. 'And how do you know it's got a picture of the Plughole Fairy on it then?'

'The man at the sweet shop said so,' said Alice.

'Well I'm not frightened, let's have a look,' said Peter. Alice gave him the piece of paper and ran behind the door. Nigel put his paws over his eyes.

Peter unfolded the piece of paper and looked at it. There was a rather badly drawn picture of a Christmas tree fairy in red crayon and scrawled under it was the word 'BOO!!'

'It's a joke,' said Peter. 'Look!'

'Do you think I'm stupid? Do you think I want to go crazy mad?' said Alice, a bit flustered, and then she added, 'well what about the Toothbrush Fairy?'

'Have you seen her then?' asked Peter.

'Of course not, nobody has,' said Alice. 'She's

much too small.'

'Oh, come on,' said Peter.

'She jumps out of the bristles when you're cleaning your teeth and makes you get holes and have to go to the dentist,' said Alice.

'That's stupid,' said Peter. 'Who told you that?'

'The man in the sweet shop.'

'That's because he doesn't want you to know it's sweets that make your teeth go bad,' said Peter.

'Now *you're* being stupid,' said Alice. 'Everybody knows that sweets are good for you, and if you don't eat lots of them you get ill and die.'

'Did the man in the sweet shop tell you that?' asked Peter.

'Yes.'

Peter went into the bathroom and ran a bath. It was a hot summer evening and the room filled up with steam. There seemed to be more than usual, great billowing swirls of it that made Peter feel as if he was floating in the sky. He lay back in the water and above him, through the mist, the ceiling seemed to be miles away and the light shone weakly like a pale sun.

Peter had had a bad week at school. The warm bath wrapped itself around him and he felt himself drifting away. His legs floated in the water, the sponges had swum down to his feet and were tickling his toes. Then he heard the voice.

'Never laugh at today what you might have on toast tomorrow,' it said.

'What?' said Peter, half waking up. 'Who said that?'

'We are all just breadcrumbs on the tablecloth of life,' said the voice.

A tiny shadowy figure appeared at the end of the bath. Peter was so sleepy and there was so much steam, all he could see was a vague shape.

'Who are you?' asked Peter. 'I can hardly see you. The steam's too thick.'

'I think you will find,' said the figure, 'that the steam is actually quite clever.'

'Come on,' said Peter. 'Who *are* you?'

'Laugh and the world laughs with you,' said the figure. 'Fry prunes and you eat alone.'

'Who are you?' said Peter for the third time.

'A rolling sausage gathers no socks,' said the ghost.

The mist cleared away from the bath, collecting in dark shadows round the walls. Peter sat up and saw the ghost on the end of the bath quite clearly.

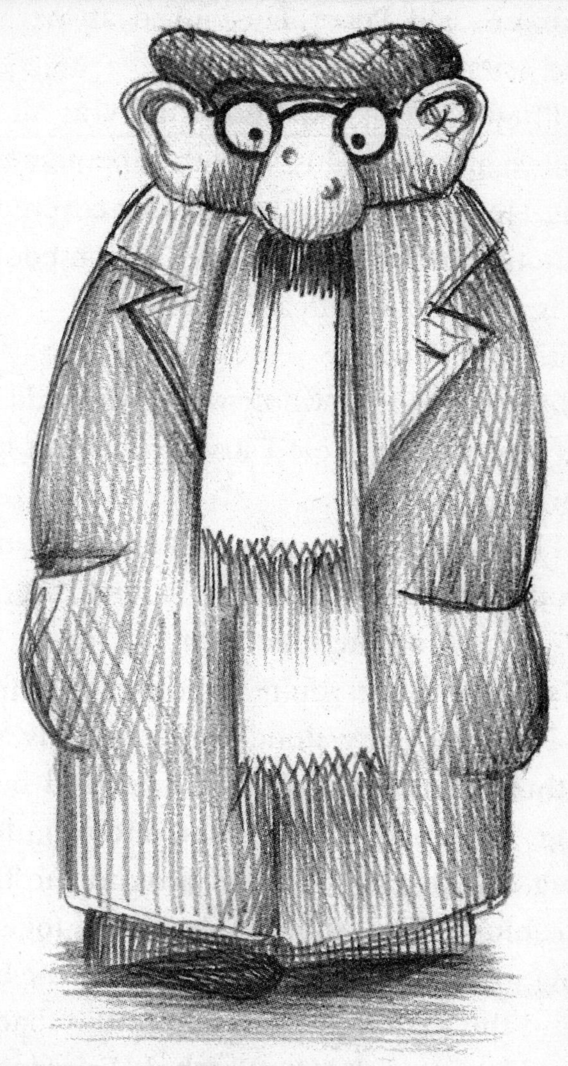

It was not what he had expected.

'Well, you're not the Plughole Fairy,' he said.

'Yes, I am,' said the figure. 'I'm Norman.'

'Norman?' said Peter. He looked at the little man and burst out laughing.

The Plughole Fairy was not a fairy at all. He didn't have any wings, just a cloth cap and a dirty raincoat. He had a big moustache that covered his entire mouth and was wearing wellington boots.

'Life is just a bowl of fleas,' he said.

'What?' said Peter.

'If all the dogs in the whole world were laid end to end,' said the Plughole Fairy, 'I wouldn't be at all surprised.'

'Am I having one of those weird dreams you get when you've been eating cheese?' asked Peter.

'No,' said the Plughole Fairy. 'Dreams are nature's way of saying, you're standing on my foot.'

The Plughole Fairy stood up, waved his arms slowly through the air, shut his eyes and began chanting. The mists swirled round and round and lightning crackled and flashed around the bathroom cabinet. The sponges huddled together shivering so hard they made little waves in the bathwater and the soap slipped away into the shadows frothing at the mouth. The Plughole Fairy looked so ridiculous, Peter couldn't take him seriously. As he chanted his trousers began to fall down over his wellingtons. He waved his arms faster and faster, took one step forward and fell into the bath.

'There's no need to swear,' said Peter.

'Swearing is nature's way of saying, help I can't swim,' said Norman. He splashed about and finally climbed onto Peter's leg looking a sorry sight. Even the sponges were laughing at him now.

'Everything you say is ridiculous,' said Peter. 'It doesn't make sense.'

'My batteries are all wet,' said Norman.

'Batteries?' said Peter.

'Yes,' said Norman. 'I can't work without batteries.'

Peter lifted the little man out of the bath and dried him off. He tried the hairdrier but it kept blowing him over, so he wrapped him up in a towel while he finished his bath. When he was dressed, he picked Norman up and sat him on a chair.

'What do you do?' he asked. 'I mean, what are you here for?'

'What are you, tomato paste with a dash of potato?' said Norman. 'Sorry, batteries nearly run down.'

He put his hands in his raincoat pockets and pulled out two tiny batteries.

'Batteries,' he said.

'Hold on,' said Peter, and ran off to his room.

He got the batteries out of his camera and took them back to Norman. The Plughole Fairy hadn't moved and Peter had to put the batteries into his pockets before anything happened.

'That's butter,' he said, pulling a sandwich out of one pocket, 'and this is margarine.'

'Do you feel better?' asked Peter.

'Well, you know how a cat's fur feels when you stroke it the wrong way?' said Norman.

'Yes,' said Peter.

'So do I,' said Norman.

'You're mad,' said Peter. 'Do you really live down the plughole?'

'Don't we all?' asked Norman.

'You are mad,' said Peter.

'Oh yes,' said Norman, 'well how do you know that the whole planet and the solar system isn't in a huge drain under a gigantic bath?'

'That's ridiculous,' said Peter.

'Oh yes?' said the Plughole Fairy, looking triumphant. 'Well you tell me where we all are. You tell me what there is outside the solar system.'

'Er, nothing,' said Peter. 'I think.'

'Well I'd rather live in a drain than in nothing,' said Norman. 'I'd rather sit down the plughole and make gurgling noises than live nowhere.'

'That noise isn't you,' said Peter. 'That's just the water running away.'

'Oh yes,' said the Plughole Fairy, 'and why do you think it's running away?'

'Because someone's pulled the plug out,' said Peter.

'No,' said the Plughole Fairy, 'it runs away because it's frightened of me making gurgling noises.'

'That's ridiculous,' said Peter and he leant into

the bath and pulled the plug out.

Nothing happened. The water just stayed where it was.

'The drain must be blocked up,' he said.

The Plughole Fairy walked under the bath and made a quick gurgling noise. The water moved as if it was shivering.

'Gurgle, gurgle, gurgle,' said the Plughole Fairy, and the water began pouring away.

'There, there, nice water,' he said and the water stopped moving.

Peter still didn't believe Norman.

'Do you mean there's someone like you down every drain in the whole world?' he said.

'Yes,' said Norman, 'my sister Agnes is over there in the washbasin. Agnes, say hello to Peter.'

'Gurgle,' said something in the sink.

'Mum and Dad are in the kitchen, Aunt Prudence is in the cloakroom and my big dog Trevor is over there down the toilet,' said Norman.

'Can I see them?' asked Peter.

'Er, it's a bit difficult at the moment,' said Norman.

'Why?'

'Erm, well, er,' said Norman.

'There's no-one there, is there?' said Peter. 'It's just you throwing your voice.'

'Throwing your voice is just nature's way of saying I've got a lovely bunch of coconuts,' said Norman.

'You are completely mad,' said Peter. 'You just talk rubbish all the time.'

'Talking rubbish is just nature's way of telling you to become an accountant,' said Norman.

'You're just a ghost mucking about,' declared Peter.

'No I'm not,' said Norman. 'I really am a fairy. I'm in disguise.'

'Well, where are your wings?' asked Peter.

'They're in the wash,' said Norman. 'I got them dirty in the garden.'

And then suddenly, and for no apparent reason, Norman started to panic. He took a battery out of his pocket and started sucking it like a baby's dummy. He ran round the room looking for somewhere to hide and finally took cover behind Peter's legs.

'All right, it's true,' he said. 'I'm not really the Plughole Fairy. I just pretended while she was off sick.'

He clung onto Peter's trouser legs and the boy could feel him shaking.

'They're going to get me,' he said. 'They'll do terrible things to me. They'll wash behind my ears and make me eat soap and make me kiss the sponges and make me swim in the toilet and make me . . .'

'Who?' asked Peter. 'Who's going to get you?'

'The Ablution Gang,' said Norman. Peter had never heard of the Ablution Gang and Norman explained that they ran the bathroom and no-one did *anything*, not even lick the soap, without their permission. 'They'll flush me away into the twilight zone,' said Norman.

There was a knocking on the door.

'OK, OK,' said Peter, 'Don't worry, I'll help you.'

The knocking on the door grew louder. Peter picked Norman up and opened it. There were three angry looking fairies standing there.

'Where is he?' demanded the tallest one.

'Where's who?' said Peter.

'Norman,' said the shortest fairy.

'What are you talking about?' said Peter, shaking his head.

'What's that you've got there?' asked the third fairy.

'This? Oh, it's Kevin my Action Man,' said Peter.

'It looks a bit like Norman to me,' said the tallest fairy.

Norman stared straight ahead without blinking while Peter jerked the little man's arms up and down.

'Twist his head right round,' said the shortest fairy, but Peter said Action Men couldn't do that and he wasn't going to break his favourite toy for three bossy fairies.

'That was close,' said Peter when they got back to his room. Norman was shaking like a leaf and couldn't speak. Peter tucked him up in his bed and went down for tea. When he got back Norman was sitting on Peter's desk eating a toffee.

'I've been thinking,' he said. 'Why don't I stay here with you?'

'Well, I don't know,' said Peter.

'Seeing the future is nature's way of telling you to become incredibly rich,' said Norman.

And he was right. Peter grew up to become a stockbroker who *always* seemed to know when the stocks and shares were going to go up or down. People thought it was odd that he took his Action Man doll everywhere with him, but then people are always jealous of someone who has their own helicopter to fly downstairs to breakfast in, in their gigantic marble castle on their own South Sea Island.

Flybogel the Witch

Flybogel the Witch was a horrific sight, even to other witches. Where they had fifty warts and pimples, she had thousands. She even had pimples on her pimples and they were all shades of purple and green, except for the yellow ones. Where other witches had two deep–sunken eyes surrounded by a sea of wrinkles, Flybogel had five eyes and two more in a box under her kitchen sink.

Some people, seeing her suddenly for the first time, had to lie down in a dark room for a week and drink a lot of whisky. If they had drunk the whisky before they looked at her, they had to lie down for a month, and often turned into bank managers.

The fact that she was so hideous was her saving grace, because as a witch she was completely useless. She had failed every single witch exam. The only spell she could do was C–A–T spells cat; but because she was so ugly, she could frighten more people than any of her cleverer sisters. She couldn't turn people into frogs. She couldn't even turn a car into a sidestreet, but she only had to look at a saucer of milk to turn it into yoghurt. She couldn't put anyone to sleep for a hundred years unless they were dead and even then, they sometimes woke up.

The other witches wondered how she had ever become a witch at all. Her mother hadn't been a witch, but her father had been a woodwork teacher and that had helped.

'Even her pointy hat is just made out of an old cornflakes box painted black,' said Elvira, Queen of the Witches.

'And as for the broomstick and black cat stuff,' said her sister Effie, 'I mean who ever heard of a witch flying round on a vacuum cleaner with a poodle called Fifi.'

Flybogel had tried a broom but all she could do was sweep the floor with it. Even the vacuum cleaner was a bit of a problem. Every time she got more than fifteen feet in the air, the plug got pulled out of the socket and she went crashing to the ground.

'At least I usually end up looking better after the crash,' she thought to herself, as she sewed her ear back on upside down, 'which is more than you can say for the ground.'

'I think we should chuck her out,' said Elvira.

'Yes, well, we all think that,' said Effie, 'but who's going to do it?'

It was the same every time they had a meeting. They all agreed Flybogel had to go, but no–one could actually face telling her.

Flybogel lived in a dark hole behind the gas meter in the cupboard under the stairs. She had lived there for as long as anyone could remember, and the family had got used to her. Everyone kept out of her way and in return for letting her live undisturbed in the cupboard, Flybogel always wore a paper bag over her head when she went through the house. No-one in the current family had ever seen what she looked like, though they had all heard rumours.

'You know what a squashed hedgehog looks like?' said Elvira to Peter's mum.

'Yes.'

'Well if you scraped up one of those and mixed it with a hundred rotten fish heads, put lipstick on it and five thousand angry boils covered with acne and black hairs and then got a hundred dripping . . . ,' said Elvira, as she sat at the kitchen table one afternoon helping Peter's mum peel potatoes.

'Yes, yes, I get the picture,' said Peter's mum.

'Wow,' said Alice, 'have you got a photo of her?'

'It's impossible,' said Elvira. 'The camera breaks even before you take the lens cap off.'

'I want to see her,' said Alice. 'I want to see what she looks like without the bag on her head.'

'I wouldn't advise it,' warned Elvira.

'Your uncle Fergus looked at her once,' said

Peter's mum. 'And he turned into a hamster.'

'What, just because she's a bit spotty?' exclaimed Alice. 'She's probably really nice.'

'It'll end in tears,' said Peter's granny.

When Alice decided to do something there was nothing much anyone could do about it. They all tried to make her see sense, but she was determined to see what Flybogel looked like for herself. Peter decided he had a very important appointment a very long way from the house and went out. Their mother thought of locking Alice in her room until she saw sense, but she knew Alice could unlock the door just by thinking hard enough. The most anyone could do was persuade her to wear two pairs of very dark sunglasses.

'Hello?' said Alice, stumbling about in the cupboard under the stairs. 'Is there anyone there?'

With the sunglasses on it was very difficult to see *anything*. She kept tripping over things and banging her shins.

'Hello,' she said again. 'Is there anyone at home?'

'No,' said a voice.

'Who's that?' asked Alice.

'Nobody,' said the voice.

'Is that Flybogel?' asked Alice.

'Maybe,' said the voice. 'Who's that?'

'It's Alice,' said Alice. 'I live in the house.'

'I know that,' said Flybogel. 'What do you want?'

'I've come to see you,' said Alice.

'It's not allowed,' said Flybogel. 'I promised I'd only come out with a paper bag on my head.'

'All right, well do that then,' said Alice. There was commotion followed by the sound of rustling paper and then silence.

'What's the matter?' said Alice.

'I've torn my paper bag,' said Flybogel.

'Never mind, just come out anyway,' insisted Alice, 'please.'

'Promise you won't be sick or turn into a hamster?'

said Flybogel.

'Of course I won't,' said Alice.

A small door at the back of the cupboard opened and the witch came out with her back to Alice. She tried to hide in the shadows but Alice turned the light on.

'Turn round then,' said Alice.

'I don't want to frighten you,' said Flybogel, but she did turn round. She was quite tall, taller than Alice's mum, and she was wearing a dress covered in brown stains. There was half a torn paper bag with the words – *Country Fresh Mushrooms* – printed on it hanging over her eyes. Alice tried not to laugh but she couldn't stop herself.

'Well, no-one's ever laughed at me before,' said Flybogel. 'They usually scream and faint.'

'It's not your face,' said Alice. 'It's the paper bag.'

So Flybogel took off the bag and Alice looked at her. She didn't scream and she didn't faint. She went up close to the witch and stared at her.

'What's the matter?' said Flybogel. 'I'm not dripping on you am I?'

'You've got dreadful spots,' said Alice.

'Tell me about it,' cried Flybogel. 'I'm hideous.' And she turned and retreated back inside her hole.

Alice followed her in and found herself in a small house. It was the untidiest place she had ever seen, far worse than her own bedroom, and that had meat pies under the bed that had been there so long they had grown fur and mutated into alien life forms. Flybogel's house was knee-deep in rubbish. Alice walked from room to room – it was everywhere. And the rubbish was all the same, millions and millions of chocolate wrappers.

EXTRA FAT
METROPOLIS
PACK
5000
STUFFO
BARS
PIGS
IN
CUSTARD
DOUBLE
LUMPY
ROLY
POLY
CHOLESTEROL
AND
COCOA
CUDDLES
BLOBBO
CAKE

'That's why you've got so many spots,' said Alice. 'I bet if you stopped eating sweets, your skin would be lovely.'

'No, it's not that,' said Flybogel. 'I had spots before I started eating sweets.'

'What did you used to eat?' said Alice.

'Lard,' said Flybogel.

'All the time?' asked Alice.

'Except Sundays,' said Flybogel. 'I used to eat grease with clotted cream on Sundays.'

'Have you ever thought of eating something like lettuce?' said Alice, 'or apples?'

'Don't be silly,' said Flybogel. 'I'm not a horse.'

Alice tried to explain about food to Flybogel. She told her all the things that were good for you and all the things that were bad for you, but she could tell the witch didn't really believe her.

'I'm sure you've got it wrong, dear,' said Flybogel. 'Fat is good for you, everyone knows that, and chocolate gives you energy.'

'No, no, that's wrong,' said Alice.

'My mother always told me to eat all my fat,' said Flybogel. Then she went off into a dream. It had been years since she had thought about her mother and it made her sad. Her mother had been as big as a house, all warm and cuddly and safe, and she had eaten sweets *and* buckets of fat all her life. And she had still been really beautiful.

'She can't have been very healthy,' said Alice.

'Yes, she was. Yes, she was,' said Flybogel.

'Could she run upstairs without getting out of breath?' asked Alice.

'Well, no she couldn't,' said Flybogel.

'See. If she'd eaten healthy food . . .' Alice started to say, but Flybogel was getting fed up and butted in.

'That's got nothing to do with it,' she snapped.

'Oh no?' said Alice. 'Well what's your explanation then?'

'We lived in a bungalow,' said Flybogel. 'We didn't have an upstairs.'

Alice would have beaten her head against the wall if it hadn't looked so sticky.

'Well all right then,' she said, 'just stay horrid and spotty and have no friends.' And with that, she left.

When she'd gone Flybogel realised that she *didn't* have any friends. Maybe Alice was right. Maybe sweets and fat and chips really were bad for you. It had been nice talking to Alice, even if she had said unkind things about her mother. She got out her photo album and looked at the pictures of her beautiful mother. She looked so warm and cuddly, and so fat. She really was incredibly fat. Flybogel's dad was in the picture too, but you could only see the top of his head sticking out of her mum's apron pocket.

'I suppose she was a bit fat,' Flybogel said to herself. 'And spotty.'

'It's funny,' she thought. 'I've never noticed her spots before. There are thousands of them.'

She put the photo album away and sat around all

afternoon feeling really miserable. It was all she could do to eat half a bucket of chocolate-covered marshmallows. They were her favourite food, she usually had them before every meal, but now they made her feel sick.

'Maybe I will cut down on the chocolates,' she thought, 'not that it will make any difference of course.'

It was a difficult week. By Tuesday Flybogel was desperate. She hadn't had any sweets for four days and her nerves were beginning to go. She searched the house from top to bottom but all she could find was a squashed toffee covered in dog hairs. By Wednesday she was so desperate she sucked all the chocolate stains off her dirty socks.

It'll save washing them, she thought.

By Friday her spots were beginning to go. You could actually see skin between them and the bathroom scales didn't run and hide behind the toilet when Flybogel went near them. She couldn't believe it. Maybe Alice was right after all.

The apples took a bit of getting used to. They were no substitute for chocolate and cake. And as for lettuce, Flybogel doubted if she'd ever like that.

As the weeks went by she grew thinner and her

skin became as clear and smooth as a baby's. Sometimes the craving for chocolate was terrible. Sometimes she had terrible dreams where she was floating in a bath of warm milk chocolate while an army of pixies dropped marshmallows into her open mouth. She would wake up covered in sweat shivering, and wander aimlessly round her home under the stairs chewing her fingers until it was morning.

All this time no-one in the house had seen her. She went out early in the morning to do her shopping and then spent the rest of the day indoors making new clothes. She was so thin now that she could make two new dresses out of one old one.

'Has anyone seen Flybogel?' said Alice. 'I keep knocking on her door but no-one answers.'

'She's probably gone off to Spell School to learn how to turn taps off,' said Elvira, Queen of the Witches.

'Or to live in a factory where they make spot cream,' said her sister Effie, and they both fell about laughing, which is something witches do all the time.

'You're horrible,' said Alice.

'Of course we're horrible, stupid,' said Elvira.

'We're witches.'

'We're meant to be horrible,' said Effie, turning the stair carpet into seven hundred jelly–fish.'

'Yeah, *really* horrible,' said Elvira, starting a thunderstorm inside the washing machine that scorched all the clothes.

'If we were nice,' said Effie, 'we'd be your mum.'

'If *you* were my mum,' said Alice, 'I'd leave home.'

She knew she could say what she liked to them because they were scared of her. All the ghosts in the house were scared of Alice because she wasn't in the slightest bit scared of any of them. There were rumours that Alice was the most powerful ghost there was, a combination of a ghost and a witch and an ogre and a bad smell all rolled into one. She wasn't, at least she didn't think she was, though she did have certain strange powers and a Barbie doll that could breathe fire.

Meanwhile Flybogel was parading in front of her bathroom mirror in a red satin dress. She was the most beautiful person she had ever seen. Her hair, which had been dull black with small animals living in it, now shone like polished ebony. Her skin, which had had more craters than the moon, was now like a golden peach. She had scraped her teeth until they sparkled and managed to dig three bags of earth from under her fingernails.

'Wow,' she said, 'I am the loveliest person in the whole world.'

At last she was ready. She stuck Fifi the poodle in her handbag, sprayed an extra coat of lacquer on her hair, and left the house. She wanted to say goodbye to Alice. After all, it was because of her that Flybogel was now how she was. But it was the middle of the night and she didn't want the other witches to see her, so she slipped quietly away.

'I'll send her a postcard,' she said on her way to the station.

A few days later she did send Alice a postcard. A week after that she sent her a flame-proof dress for her Barbie doll. The third week she sent her a computer and every week after that a present arrived for Alice. Sometimes it was a box of chocolates, sometimes flowers. And once Alice got a holiday for two in the paradise of her choice, and once a red sports car.

Flybogel never went back to the house by the sea but everyone saw her on television a few weeks later, a tall elegant star in a new soap opera. In fact, they saw her twice a week, for years and years.

'You know, it's amazing what they can do with make up on TV,' said Elvira, Queen of the Witches. 'You can't see her three extra eyes at all.'

The Sweet Little Old Lady

One day a very, very old lady turned up at the house. She had been old when Peter's granny had been a child and no-one could really believe that she was still alive.

'It's just a matter of lifestyle,' said Great-Great Aunt Edna as she swallowed her fifteenth oyster. 'You have to lead a balanced life,' she said as she polished off her fifth glass of champagne and lit a cigar.

'Balanced?' said Peter's mum.

'Yes,' said Great-Great Aunt Edna, 'much too much of everything.'

'I thought you'd gone years ago,' said Peter's granny.

'Gone, gone?' said Great-Great Aunt Edna. 'For goodness sake, I'm only a hundred and twenty.'

'Well, where have you been all these years?' asked Peter's granny.

'Everywhere,' said Great-Great Aunt Edna. 'Last week I was white-water rafting with the marines and before that I was in the round the world yacht race.'

'Wow!' said Peter. 'Did you win?'

'No,' said Great-Great Aunt Edna, 'I didn't realise it was for sailing boats, I was rowing so I was a bit behind. Mind you, I wasn't last.'

'What else have you done?' said Alice.

Great-Great Aunt Edna talked for hours, long past bedtime, right into the middle of the night. She told them about pushing a shopping trolley full of custard up Everest, about swimming the English Channel in a ball-gown, about flying over the North Pole in a hot air balloon knitted out of spaghetti, and about discovering Mammoths in a Siberian forest. Peter's granny snorted and muttered under her breath telling everyone, as usual, about how it would all end in tears, but no-one took any notice. They just kept sending her off to the kitchen to make cups of tea while Great-Great Aunt Edna carried on describing her adventures.

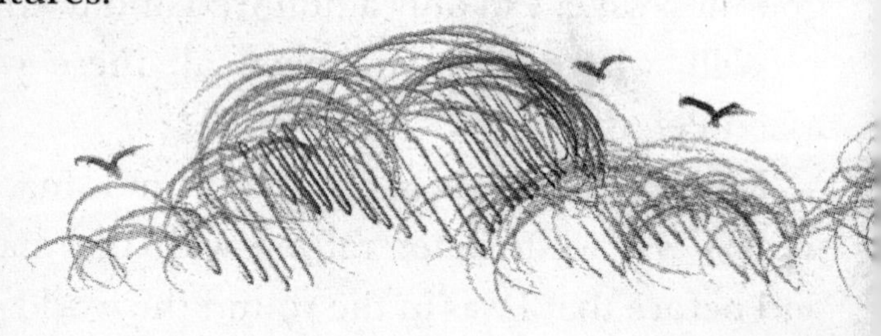

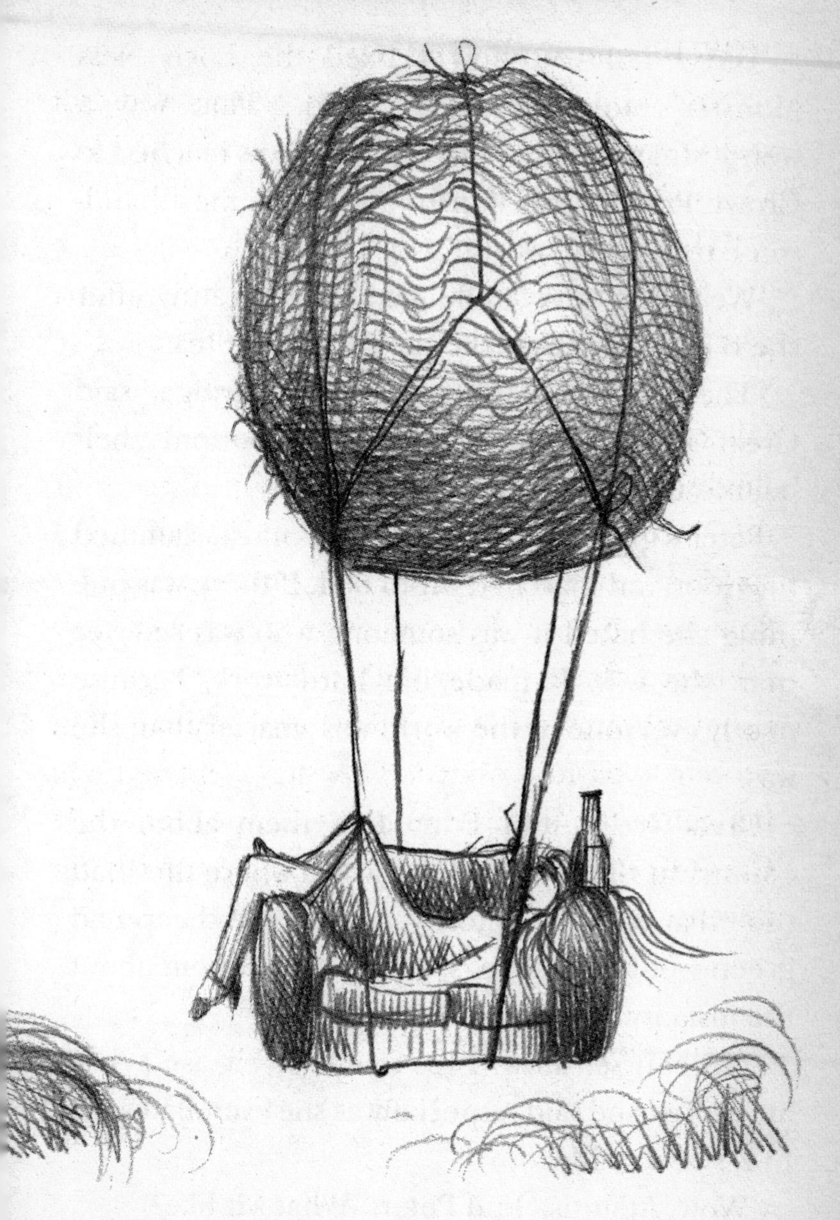

'Did I tell you how I fixed the Loch Ness Monster's toothache?' she said. 'That was a wonderful year. That was the year I was married to Crown Prince Otto Von Inkmark, the most handsome man in the world.'

'We've run out of milk,' said Peter's granny, after she'd been sent to make the fifth pot of tea.

'There's a bottle in the back of the fridge,' said Great-Great Aunt Edna, 'on the bottom shelf behind the cabbage.'

Peter's granny made a final pot of tea, slammed the door and marched off to bed. If there was one thing she hated it was someone who was smarter than she was. It made life hard work, because nearly everyone in the world was smarter than she was.

Great-Great Aunt Edna told them about the country at the centre of the world where they had the great volcano factories, and all the sheep had green wool and six legs, and she told them about the lost city of Atlantis.

'Of course, now I've found it, it isn't lost anymore,' she said, especially as she even had an A to Z street guide.

'Wow, Atlantis,' said Peter. 'What's it like?'

'Wet.'

She told them about the time she had crossed the Sahara on stilts made out of chocolate, and how she had once made an omelette with twenty-three thousand eggs that had fed the entire population of a remote Himalayan country for a whole winter, and how they had made her a goddess for saving their lives and let her marry the most handsome man in the country.

'That was after I divorced my nineteenth husband, Lord Tristram Forecourt-Wheelbrace, the nineteenth Earl of Frinton-Le-Gateau-On-sea,' said Great-Great Aunt Edna. 'You must have heard of him, he invented underwater yoghurt.'

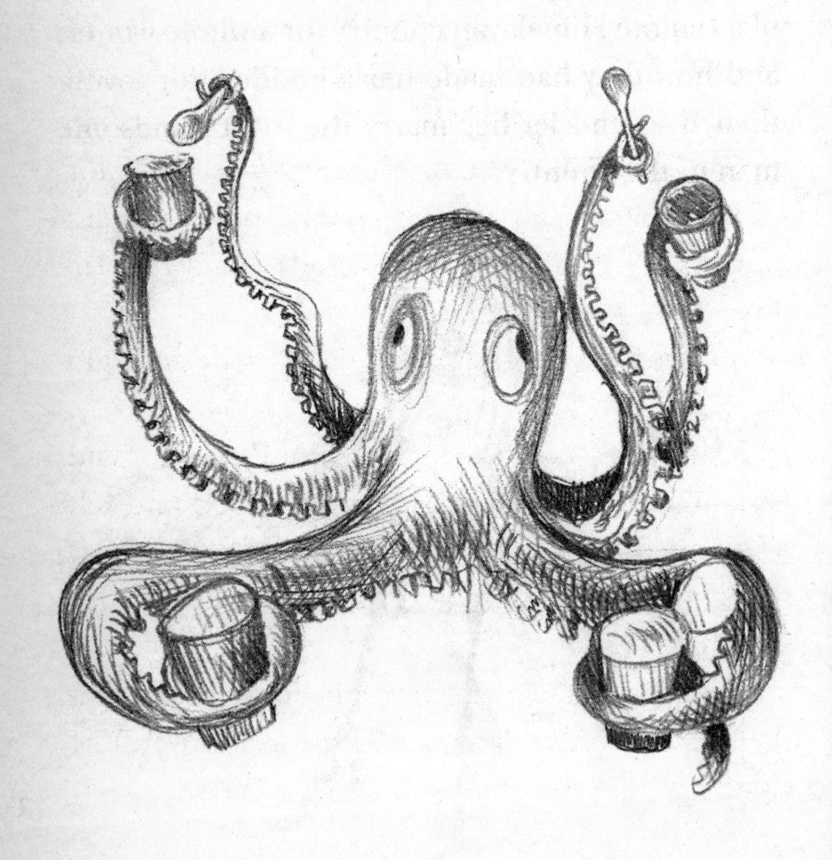

By two in the morning everyone's head was filled up with amazing stories. Peter and Alice thought that Great-Great Aunt Edna was the most amazing person they had ever met. They could hardly believe they were related to someone who had won the decathlon in the Olympics at the age of seventy the same year as she was light-weight boxing champion of the world. It was amazing, especially as she had also got the Nobel Prize for Literature that year and won a waterproof camera in the Kellogs Cornflakes competition to draw a cornflake.

'So what's the best thing you've ever done?' said Alice.

'I suppose that has to be coming here,' said Great-Great Aunt Edna. Everyone smiled and felt all warm inside, but then the old lady said, 'and getting you all to believe all these ridiculous stories.'

And she floated away through the dining room wall leaving only a laugh and an ash-tray full of cigar.

The Plughole Fairy 2

Last week as I sat in the bath
I thought I heard someone laugh,
A gurgling deep in the drain.
I listened and heard it again.

The sponge shook and shivered in fright.
And the soap slipped away in the night.
Then a voice below the plug said,
'I'll get you tonight in your bed.'

Then the fairy from down the drain
Put a dripping tap in my brain.
And I travelled the world in my dreams
Through rivers and oceans and streams.

I sailed over all the seven seas
And swam through waves tall as trees
To surf the great internet.
When I woke up the bed was all wet.

The Plughole Fairy 2

Ghost Chickens in the Sky

Ethel the chicken kept falling through the clouds. The other chickens didn't seem to have any problem with it but they'd all been dead a lot longer than her. There was even a turkey as fat as a sheep that could do it but Ethel just couldn't get the hang of it.

'There's nothing there to actually sit on,' she said. 'It's all just fluff.'

'You're just not doing it right,' said one of the other hens. 'You're just being too heavy.'

'But I *am* heavy,' said Ethel. 'I'm a fat chicken.'

'No, no, you're a ghost now,' said the other hen. 'You shouldn't weigh anything.'

'She just hasn't been dead long enough,' said another old hen. 'It takes a bit of getting used to.'

Then Ethel remembered. She had been so old and so tired that every bone and muscle in her body had ached. She had gone into the house and climbed the stairs to heaven and now all her aches and pains had vanished. Now she was young again.

Blodwen was the oldest chicken of all. She had been a ghost since Roman times and had even laid an egg for Julius Caesar. She floated over and gave Ethel a gentle shove upwards.

'You just have to stretch your wings and let yourself float away,' she said, and she was right. All around her Ethel could see white chickens sailing through the sky like a huge cloud of cotton wool.

'Just think light,' said Blodwen.

In life, chickens are great lumpy awkward creatures that flap and waddle everywhere. If they grit their beaks and really try they can get a few feet off the ground, but the world record for chicken flight is less than the long-jump record for a snail.

In life, chickens are the joke of the bird world. Even the scruffiest sparrows laugh at them. But when they become ghosts, all that changes. They soar like the wind. They gather in great white clouds and circle the world for ever, rising and falling and following the sun. Slowly as the centuries pass they lose their feathers until they are invisible, but even then, the chickens are still there, millions and millions of them. Most of Blodwen had vanished.

'It's a good job we do become transparent,' she said. 'Otherwise we would have blocked out the sun years ago.'

'It's all very confusing,' said Ethel.

'It's all right,' said Blodwen. 'I'll take you under my wing.'

'Where is it?'asked Ethel, confused.

It certainly did take some getting used to. The floating bit wasn't actually too bad. After a few days Ethel was diving and swooping with the best of them, and after a week she felt young again. The worst thing was never eating. She knew she didn't *have* to eat now she was a ghost but it had been her greatest pleasure. All her life, every day, she had scratched about in the earth with her feet and then jumped back, head to one side, to see what she had uncovered.

'I miss that,' said Ethel. 'It was the most important thing I ever did.'

'I know,' said Blodwen, 'I miss it too.'

'Couldn't we still do it,' said Ethel, 'at night when no–one's looking?'

'It's a bit difficult when you're a ghost,' said Blodwen. 'One good scrape and you fly up in the air doing a somersault.'

'Have you tried it then?' asked Ethel.

'Oh yes,' said Blodwen. 'We all have.'

'Well, I'd like to have a go,' said Ethel.

'It's no good,' said Blodwen, shaking her head from side to side.

'How about if we all tried it together?' said Ethel. 'Or we sat on each other's shoulders? It would make us heavier.'

'No it wouldn't,' said Blodwen. 'Nothing plus nothing equals nothing.'

'Well, how about if two of us sat on each other's shoulders?' asked Ethel, who was not good at maths.

Blodwen muttered something very rude in Welsh but in the end, for the sake of peace and quiet, they all agreed to have a go at scratching for worms. They waited until it was dark so no–one would see them, and landed in the middle of a field.

'The grass is a bit long,' said Ethel, 'but it'll do.'

Six hundred ghost chickens lined up in rows of threes and made a big circle. They locked wings together and then six hundred more stood on their shoulders and six hundred more on theirs. When they were ready, Ethel shouted, 'NOW!!' and they started scratching.

'This is ridiculous,' said Blodwen, half an hour later. 'I haven't found a single worm.'

They flew somewhere else and tried again, but it was just the same. They didn't find a single worm anywhere.

'I saw an ant,' said one old hen.

'Look,' said Blodwen. 'Enough is enough. Every year this happens. Some new ghosts think they can still scratch up worms.'

'Maybe we should try a different country,' said Ethel.

'No,' said Blodwen, 'it won't make any difference. And anyway, if a big fat slimy worm fell out of the sky, you wouldn't be able to eat it. You're a ghost. Your beak would just pass right through it and it wouldn't even notice.'

'I suppose you're right,' said Ethel.

As the morning sun crept up over the trees the eighteen hundred chickens floated up into the sky and became a cloud once more.

'Still,' said Ethel, 'you have to admit. All those big circles we made in the corn fields do look rather pretty.'

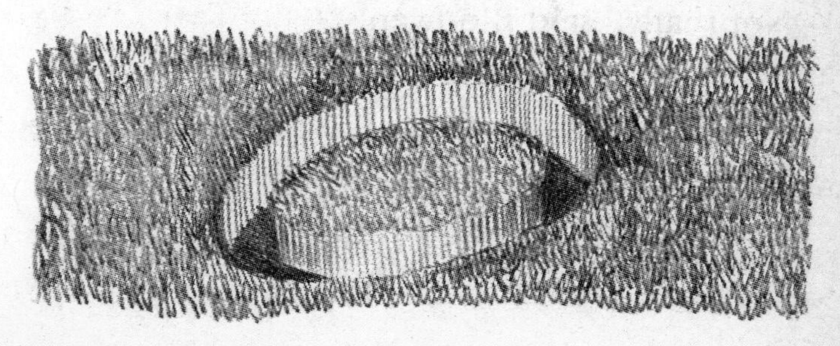

The months passed and Ethel stopped thinking about worms. She became part of a small cloud and spent most of her time floating about over Italy. Sometimes in the summer they drifted north, across France and over the English channel, but it was always very crowded over England. There were millions and millions of chicken ghosts drifting about everywhere.

The years passed and Ethel drifted right over the town where she had lived. She thought she might find her husband Eric, but in a world with over five–hundred–million chicken ghosts she knew it wasn't very likely.

'Have you ever met anyone you used to know?' she asked Blodwen.

'Oh yes,' said Blodwen. 'I met you yesterday.'

'So you did,' said Ethel. 'And the day before.'

'Probably,' said Blodwen. 'I can't remember.'

'It's a small world isn't it?' said Ethel.

'Not really,' said Blodwen.

was a terrible feeling being so restless. Ethel
dn't remember when she had felt like it
re. She hated being a ghost.
f only I could find Eric,' she thought. What a
derful cockerel he had been, so tall and bossy
with such lovely tail feathers. After thirty years
el could still remember how proud she had felt
y morning when he had flown onto the shed
f and crowed his head off. She could remember
running away just before next door's upstairs
low opened and the bucketful of water came
g out. Eric may have been big and beautiful
like Blodwen, he had also been very, very
id. Every morning, just after his third
k-a-doodle-doo, he had been soaked to the
. The window opened, Eric looked up at
noise and got the water right in his face. They
been such happy days. Even after Eric had
e and she had been on her own living in an old
ge box, it had been better than this.
here is an old Chinese saying that says if you
d on top of a mountain with your mouth open
ong enough, a roast duck will fly into it. Ethel
't know about this, but something told her that
e floated around the world with her eyes open

And that was how it was every day. Hundreds upon hundreds of chickens drifting through the sky having meaningless conversations over and over again. They knew they were doing it, but there didn't seem to be much else to do. One cloud in America tried to bring a bit of variety into their deaths by talking about knitting patterns and wall-paper, but no–one knew what knitting patterns or wallpaper were, so it wasn't very successful.

'I remember hearing some humans talking about "knitting patterns" once,' said an old Rhode Island Red. 'They did it for hours and hours.'

'And was it interesting?' said another.

'I don't know,' said the first chicken. 'It was like the brown gravy they poured on me after I became a ghost, it went completely over my head.'

'Is this it?' asked Ethel. 'Is this how it's going to be for ever and ever?'

'What do you mean?' said Blodwen.

'Is this all we do,' said Ethel, 'just float around the world, wittering on about nothing?'

'Well,' said Blodwen, 'what's wrong with that? There's no–one to bother us, no-one to try and dip us in toasty breadcrumbs. What more do you want?'

And that was how it was every day. Hundreds upon hundreds of chickens drifting through the sky having meaningless conversations over and over again. They knew they were doing it, but there didn't seem to be much else to do. One cloud in America tried to bring a bit of variety into their deaths by talking about knitting patterns and wallpaper, but no–one knew what knitting patterns or wallpaper were, so it wasn't very successful.

'I remember hearing some humans talking about "knitting patterns" once,' said an old Rhode Island Red. 'They did it for hours and hours.'

'And was it interesting?' said another.

'I don't know,' said the first chicken. 'It was like the brown gravy they poured on me after I became a ghost, it went completely over my head.'

'Is this it?' asked Ethel. 'Is this how it's going to be for ever and ever?'

'What do you mean?' said Blodwen.

'Is this all we do,' said Ethel, 'just float around the world, wittering on about nothing?'

'Well,' said Blodwen, 'what's wrong with that? There's no–one to bother us, no-one to try and dip us in toasty breadcrumbs. What more do you want?'

'I don't know,' said Ethel, 'something.'

They were floating across open countryside towards a beautiful sunset. The fields were criss-crossed with thick hedges and trees full of chattering birds settling down for the night. Thin lines of smoke drifted up from a row of cottages. And beyond the houses, the land slipped down to the sea. It was so peaceful and so beautiful, and Ethel hated it.

'I'm bored,' she announced.

'Don't be stupid,' said Blodwen. 'You're a chicken, you're too stupid to get bored.'

'That doesn't make sense,' said Ethel. 'First you tell me not to be stupid, then you tell me I'm stupid.'

'Don't be stupid,' said Blodwen. She was very stupid herself and completely confused, but she knew that chickens didn't get bored, or at least they weren't supposed to.

'Look at the sunset,' she said. 'It's so beautiful.'

'It's boring,' said Ethel. 'I've seen it a thousand times and it's boring.'

It was a terrible feeling being so restless. Ethel couldn't remember when she had felt like it before. She hated being a ghost.

'If only I could find Eric,' she thought. What a wonderful cockerel he had been, so tall and bossy and with such lovely tail feathers. After thirty years Ethel could still remember how proud she had felt every morning when he had flown onto the shed roof and crowed his head off. She could remember too, running away just before next door's upstairs window opened and the bucketful of water came flying out. Eric may have been big and beautiful but like Blodwen, he had also been very, very stupid. Every morning, just after his third cock–a–doodle–doo, he had been soaked to the skin. The window opened, Eric looked up at the noise and got the water right in his face. They had been such happy days. Even after Eric had gone and she had been on her own living in an old orange box, it had been better than this.

There is an old Chinese saying that says if you stand on top of a mountain with your mouth open for long enough, a roast duck will fly into it. Ethel didn't know about this, but something told her that if she floated around the world with her eyes open

The End

Ghost Chickens in the Sky

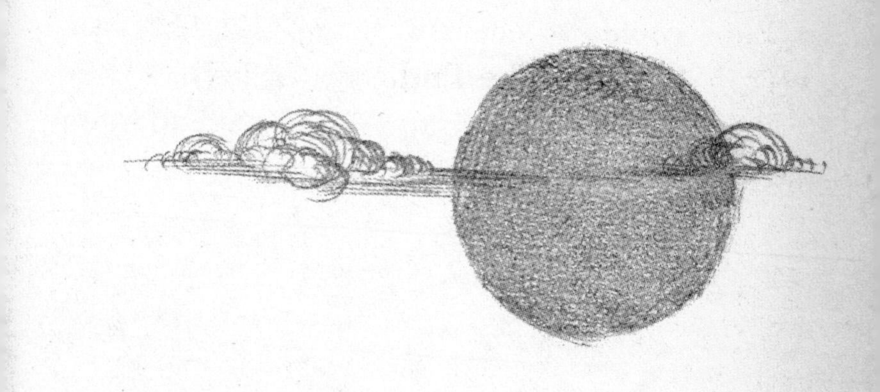

his head to one side, peered down at her and said, 'Who are you?'

Ethel couldn't believe it. It *was* Eric. She was certain. How could he have forgotten her?

'Just kidding,' he said, and they floated off into the sunset, the smallest cloud in the sky.

for long enough, she would eventually find Eric. And one day, she did.

He was part of a small cloud over Tasmania. He had been blown there years ago in a storm and had been going round in circles ever since. It was a tiny cloud, no more than a couple of hundred ghosts, just big enough to annoy people when they looked up into the sky hoping to see it clear blue from side to side.

Quite how Ethel ended up in Tasmania is not certain, but eventually she did. Her cloud floated over a snow-covered mountain and down into a beautiful valley. Then they surrounded the small cloud that Eric lived in.

It had been a hundred years since Ethel had seen Eric but as soon as she heard his voice, it all came flooding back. Their eyes met across the cloud and Ethel's heart skipped a beat which was difficult considering it had stopped beating altogether nearly a century ago.

'Eric,' she said, 'is that you?'

She looked deep into Eric's eyes. They still shone dark like polished coal just how she remembered them. All the loneliness and boredom of the past years slipped away as she floated to his side. He put